THROUGH MYSTIC WATERS

TABATHA WAYBRIGHT

THROUGH MYSTIC WATERS

By Tabatha Waybright

Published by Vesperinikin Publishing

Tuttle, OK

ISBN-13: 979-8-9900537-2-4

Editor: Rob Waybright

Cover Deign and Layout: Rob Waybright

Illustrator: Scarlett Lewis

Visit the author's website at www.tabathaswaybright.com

First Edition

Library of Congress Control Number: 2026914680

VERSES

To my fellow pilgrims young and old. May we always follow Him.

. . .We must help the weak, remembering the words the Lord Jesus himself said: "It is more blessed to give than to receive."
(Acts 20:35)

Even small children are known by their actions
(Proverbs 20:11a)

Glossary

Mystic — "deeply spiritual."

Rory Tibbets — "red king" and "mighty warrior."

Socorro — "help" or "relief."

Ailsa — "supernatural victory."

Hamish — "supplanter"

Kristal — "ice"

Murdock — "protector of the sea."

Amazing Grace - Lyrics by John Newton

Amazing grace! how sweet the sound,
That saved a wretch; like me!
I once was lost, but now am found,
Was blind, but now I see.

'Twas grace that taught my heart to
fear,
And grace my fears relieved;
How precious did that grace appear
The hour I first believed!

The Lord hath promised good to me,
His word my hope secures;
He will my shield and portion be
As long as life endures.

When we've been there ten thousand
years,
Bright shining as the sun,
We've no less days to sing God's praise
Than when we first begun.

Dedicated with much love, to my parents.

They would have been so proud to know I have become an author.

So, Rose and Houston, this book is for you.

I wish you were still here to read it!!

Acknowledgments

Special thanks to all my family for all the help, love and support!
Robert, Jessica, Rob and Mariah. Each of you has had a significant role in my book writing and developing process. I love you.
And last but not least, to my advanced readers, Jessica and Jan Evans, your help is very much appreciated!

CHAPTER 1

LAD OVERBOARD

Rory Tibbetts awoke to the piercing call of a sea gull. He jerked himself up to a sitting position in the wet sand and spewed out salt water like a geyser spews steam. He gasped, coughing spasmodically to rid himself of the water from the sea. Time seemed to stand still for the struggling teen; his body robbed of oxygen. His head was spinning and his icy bare toes cramped to the point they curled.

After what seemed like an eternity of painful coughs, he recovered enough to glance around, only to realize he couldn't see! He yanked at a wad of seaweed that blocked his view. It had wound itself into his long, matted hair and hung slimy and putrid in his face. Yuck! He stood up and grabbed the slimy stuff, ridding himself of most of it. *Where am I?* he pondered. It was then that shadows from the past few days began to flash across his mind. His heart began a painful gallop in his chest, as he remembered the angry face of his captain!

He quickly looked around him for any signs of a ship. When he didn't see any, he released an audible sigh of relief. Above, seabirds alerted him to the fact he was still alive as they dove for their breakfast. He watched them circle and dive in the stringy sunbeams that danced on the waves. He felt the frigid breeze on his cheeks, and he drank in the fishy smell of the sea. He was alive! But before he could celebrate, he realized he was in full view of the lighthouse! He must hide!

He snatched up the lifebuoy and used the last bit of his energy to scurry across the sand, like a crab escaping a predator. The rocky ridge nearby would provide the perfect hiding spot. He moved toward it as fast as his weary body would take him. When he was safely hidden behind the ridge, he slid to the ground. He waited until he could breathe naturally again, before he took inventory of his condition. His legs wibble-wobbled like jelly when he stood up. He was shoe-less. His pants were ripped at the knees and stained with mud and blood, and his hands were scraped and sore. Considering what he'd been through, though, he could deal with these minor injuries! He was alive and free! He shook his head, and more seaweed and sand flew out of his hair. He finger-combed through it to rid himself of the rest of the debris. Then he turned his head from side to side draining the last bits of water from his ears.

Tibbetts closed his eyes and leaned back against the rock. The sun's rays seeped into his torn, chilled skin, warming him a bit. But jeopardy was nothing new to the teen. He'd been through it the past few years. Unwanted thoughts of his recent past flooded his memory. *The pirates, ugh!* He had deemed himself lucky when he first secured a job aboard a large tramp steamer. *Ha! What bad luck that turned out to be!*

Tibbetts was promised three meals a day, a place to lay his head, and a paycheck once a month. It seemed like a fortune to the homeless lad. The vessel even had a cool name, the *Sea Witch.* The lure of adventure and hope of stability had clouded his judgment. He assumed it was just another fishing vessel. There were many that had docked in the bay near Liverpool, where he lived. So, he grabbed at the chance of work without any knowledge of what he was about to take on.

He'd laughed as he sailed away from the city where he had known nothing but hunger and poverty, since his only relative, his dad, had died suddenly a few years back. Without any means to support himself, he'd lived on the streets, forging scraps from garbage bins and lifting fruit or tidbits from grocery marts.

His mum had died when he was just a wee lad, and his dad had raised him. During those early years, he lacked for nothing; he even attended a private school. But when his dad took ill and died suddenly, he found himself alone and without a guardian. The authorities stepped in and sent him to a boarding school. But luckily, he escaped before he got there and returned to the streets of Liverpool. He'd heard all the horror stories about those places. According to rumors, they locked you in and made you work long hours, with little schooling and even less food. So, he took to the streets, scrounging for food and shelter and hiding from the authorities.

But he'd grown to hate his fate. It was so different than the privileged life he'd lived as a banker's son. He found himself at the mercy of gangs and criminals, who promised everything and delivered nothing. He refused to join them, and the drug-filled, violent life they led. But that too proved to be dangerous. There was safety in numbers, and he was all alone.

One day while scrounging for his breakfast, he chanced upon a bloke that told him about the job on the tramp steamer. He dropped everything and ran. He could not believe he was first in line! When offered, he took it immediately! About fifteen other teens were hired that day. They were all elated at landing the job.

Tibbetts was responsible for cleaning the decks, docking and undocking the vessel, and winding up ropes and nets. Simple tasks he could do! But he soon learned it was not as easy as all that. The other mates working aboard the vessel were grumpy and didn't mind back handing him on a whim!

They were dirty, smelled awful, and they stole from each other, just as they had done on the streets.

Then one night while winding back the nets, Tibbetts overheard the captain on his radio making drug deals. He couldn't help but hear since the captain was cursing at someone at the top of his lungs!

The gall of disappointment choked him. This was no better than the life he had left! If he was caught aboard a vessel like this, he would be locked away somewhere! Or even worse, he might be killed by the drug lords or his shipmates. He'd already tasted blood one time too many as they showed their violent side. He was determined from that time forward to get off this ship.

But they had been at sea for almost three months. They were far away from any shore. Nothing but water for as far as you could see and beyond.

He was not informed of what port they were headed for, or when they would arrive. He was not informed of anything except where to drop the nets and when to drag them back in. But he made plans as he worked. He would get off or die trying. He hoped it was the former.

Stealing a lifeboat was out of the question. The noise it made as it inflated would alert his shipmates. Jumping into the icy water without land in sight was certain death and other than growing wings and flying away, he was out of ideas.

In the meantime, Tibbetts did his job as best as he could, dodging the blows from the mates when he was able. He stayed to himself and hid away, planning his escape. But he was prompt to appear when orders were barked at him! He had seen other disobedient lads thrown into the sea by the angry captain!

Even though he was fed regularly with the other hands, the food was mostly lukewarm fish stew without any seasonings, stale bread and occasionally a citrus drink. But the fact that it was provided three times a day was a plus, and he noticed he was growing stronger. That, and the hard work, had improved his muscle strength.

Months one and two went by without any pay. When he got up nerve enough to ask about it, the captain cursed at him and threatened to throw him overboard for his cheekiness! Tibbetts backed away.

One evening, Tibbetts was daydreaming as he wound up the nets. The sunsets on the sea were magnificent. He was mesmerized as he watched the reds, yellows and oranges dance on the gray-blue water. He was tempted by its magical allure to step out and glide to where the sun and sea kissed each other goodnight!

In these quiet times, he felt a spark of hope. Maybe the being that orchestrated this magnificent sunset could work a miracle in his life. *Maybe.* Did security and peace exist out there somewhere? His heart hoped so. He'd love a few companions to laugh with, or to even struggle through life with. Even though he was surrounded by sailors, he had no one who cared a wee iota about him. He felt so alone.

As he continued his work, the gray of evening was swallowed by the ink of night. A half-crescent moon started its assent, and the dim twinkles of the heavenly bodies became visible. He sat there alone in the darkness for the longest time, thinking about the One who created it all. His mum had told him about a loving creator when he was a wee lad. But where was He now? He needed His help, but there was nothing but silence. *Wait, what was that?*

In the distance a small flicker of light appeared, disappeared and then appeared again. It was regular, repeating. Then it dawned on him, it was a beam, from a lighthouse! Shore could not be that far away! He watched in amazement as the wee light morphed in size, swallowing the darkness around it. As it gradually grew larger, he realized they were headed right for it!

He leaned as far as he could over the railing and watched. It was still except for his hair blowing in the wind. He heard the boisterous sounds of laughter and singing from below, and he knew the mates were slopping down the hard liquor. They'd had a successful day fishing and used that as an excuse to party. He'd wait until they passed out to make his move.

When it finally grew quiet, he crept below and peered at the mates. Not a soul awake! Now was his chance if he was brave enough to take it! He crept over to where a lifebuoy hung on the railing. Creeping over as quiet as the stars above, he removed it.

He was already wearing a life jacket (one of the few rules the mates actually followed), so the only thing else he needed, was the buoy for protection in the sea.

The light was growing larger and larger as they neared the shore. It was time to jump! *Someone at the stern better wake up and put this vessel on course or we'll crash into the rocky reef! H*e thought, as he grew more alarmed.

Then he heard the the sound of the engine brake. Finally, someone was at the helm! But before the ship was put into reverse, Tibbetts placed the ring around his waist, took a deep breath and jumped! He pushed away from the ship with a strong kick and began to swim. He kept watch for activity on the boat. But all was quiet. He thanked his lucky stars that no one saw or heard him go into the sea!

Wait! Suddenly the ship was alive with dozens of red, glowing, eyes peering at him! *What's that?* he gasped.

But they quickly became unimportant as the cold, thick waves did their best to devour him. He fought against the demonic water all night and with his last bit of energy, he flung himself out of the water and onto the sandy beach. Nearing hypothermia and exhaustion, he passed out. The darkness hid his limp body from the elderly watchman who snoozed in the watchtower.

Unbeknownst to Tibbetts, an angel spread her thick robe over the lad's frigid body and stayed by his side through the long night. Her breath provided a warm breeze that kept his blood flowing. Just before dawn, she disappeared, although never letting him out of her sight. The guardian angel had finished her job for the moment. But as it is with all young lads, it wouldn't be finished for long!

CHAPTER 2

FINDING BREAKFAST

"What now?" Tibbetts questioned aloud, shivering. He didn't even know where he was! *Am I even still in Europe?* He shook his head trying to think clearly but he was clueless. He searched the surrounding area hoping it would speak up and tell him what he needed to know. His eyes stopped on the lighthouse. Right now, it was his only source of help. Its beacon had saved him last night, but was he ready to face whoever was inside? They were sure to send him back to Liverpool!

He reached into his pockets looking for his ID and passport. All he found was wet sand. It was all lost when he jumped into the sea!

He dreaded risking an encounter with strangers and the unknown. But he had to do something and soon! His belly was cramping from lack of food, and his mouth was so dry it felt like cactus could grow on his tongue!

Feeling desperate, he stepped out from behind the rocks. That's when he saw it, a massive castle on the ridge overlooking the sea. It was no more than a kilometer away! The castle flags were blowing in the wind from the turrets. And he recognized them, they were Scottish flags for sure! Had he made it all the way to the Scottish islands?

Now he had a choice, lighthouse or castle. Hmm, but what was that noise? It was rapidly growing louder so he turned toward the sound. A quad bike with two aboard was approaching rapidly. He ducked behind his rocky overhang to get out of their sight. The quad bike stopped near the lighthouse. When they killed the engine, he peeked out and saw two kids, a lad and lass.

~

Socorro and Ailsa were doing their morning chores. But today, they were running late. Gee would be hungry! They flew as fast as they could without upsetting the food basket and skidded to a stop near the lighthouse door. Ailsa slipped off and hurried in, setting the basket on the counter of the galley. It was loaded with breakfast scones, egg, sausage and cheese sandwiches, and a container of mixed fruit. A tall thermos of hot tea was also planted on the counter.

"Oi, Gee! Breakfast is served!" she shouted, as she pulled a platter from the cupboard and laid out the food. She opened the thermos and poured out a cup of the hot amber liquid, then mixed in a generous helping of cream and sugar, just like Gee liked it.

Gee was the elderly keeper of the lighthouse and was like a grandfather to her and the other kids on the island.

She didn't wait around for him to come, though. He was quite elderly, and he took his time descending the stairs and usually came down when his work schedule allowed.

She grabbed the basket, ran back out, and jumped on the quad bike.

"Hey, Ailsa. Let's take a quick tour up the beach!" Socorro shouted as soon as she was securely on the four wheeled vehicle. What he really meant was, 'Let's go see if the animals are around!' Socorro gunned the engine, jerking Ailsa's head back against the seat. Dirt and gravel flew as the machine all but launched like a rocket headed for outer space!

Tibbetts quietly watched the whole thing from the nearby rocks.

The frigid morning wind bit at their cheeks as they sped as far as they could up the beach, until the rock overhangs and extended waterways blocked them. They skidded to a stop, the tires of the machine eating up the sand and spewing it into the air. Good thing Ailsa was used to Socorro's crazy driving, or she would have been thrown!

"Ach, you could be a wee bit more careful, ya know," she scolded in her sweet Scottish accent. "I'm nae beyond injury noo, am I?"

Socorro laughed at her supposed "outrage." If Ailsa had been driving, she wouldn't have done a thing differently. They'd been good friends for a couple of years now and they both loved living on the edge. Ailsa pushed her glasses up on her nose and shook her strawberry-blond curls away from her eyes. For at least ten of her twelve years she had struggled with her wild hair. But Socorro had told her that her curls were one of her best assets. They gave her that 'wild and free' look that matched her personality.

Ailsa had grown up tremendously in the past two years that Socorro had known her. He couldn't help but notice how the wee girl (with glasses that seemed too big for her face) had grown into those glasses and how she had taken on a charm, as she shook off the wee and innocent and stepped into the misty murk of puberty. Her azure eyes were framed by long lashes that curled on her delicate sun-kissed cheeks. She didn't wear make-up, because nature had been kind to Ailsa, and none was needed.

Although she seemed oblivious to it, Socorro couldn't help but notice she'd been blessed with a natural beauty that had heightened as she grew. There was not quite two years difference in their ages, and two years ago he wouldn't have thought twice about the girl. But something was slowly changing between them. Two years didn't seem like too much of a gap. Anyway, her wit matched his.

They stopped near the shoreline and shed their shoes and socks. But they kept their eyes on the sea, trying to spy a few whale tails or dolphins in the waves.

Socorro lifted his hand to his forehead, shielding his eyes from the rising sun as he strained to see the animals. The white capped waves danced toward them, then just as suddenly were drawn back by the ever-rolling tide. The water was shallow at the beach but was nearly bottomless near the rocks and cliffs, and the creatures loved to hang out there. The kids were bound to see some soon.

"Let's climb up the cliffs to get a better view," Ailsa shouted. "Won't hurt none to take a wee peek."

Socorro raced ahead of her, scampering up the rocks. They were rough and jagged from years of seawater pestering their existence, creating tall spires which made for many sturdy handholds. He had become quite adept at climbing, after exploring the island with Ailsa over the past two years. *Oh, the adventures they'd had!* From poachers to shipwrecks, to the friendships with the sweet Scottish coos of the highlands! And of course, the puffins and other exotic birds on the island.

Much to his chagrin, even though Socorro had had a head start, it was the wee and agile Ailsa that reached the top first. Socorro threw up his hands in a 'really, I can't believe she did it again' jester. Ailsa giggled, then leaned over the edge as far as she dared and exclaimed loudly, "I see them. Look, dolphins below!" The wind whipped her hair and clothes as it swirled about her. Socorro felt threatened by it as a gust pushed him closer to the edge.

"Step back, Ailsa, the winds are strong, and you are too close!" He reached over and grabbed the back of her thick jumper and pulled her away from the edge. She was always freaking him out! *Didn't the girl have any fear? A wee bit of caution is healthy,* he thought. He started to remind her of this, but she turned to him laughing and shook her finger at him.

"Ach, Socorro, you remind me of my mum. If you had an apron on, you'd be her twin!" She turned and ran, knowing he would pretend to clobber her. She scurried across the top of the rock, hopping from foothold to foothold, causing Socorro heart palpitations!

He hurried behind her, laughing and doing his best to keep up. Miraculously, the two made it back to the beach and the vehicle. It was past time to head home before their parents sent out the posse. They were allowed to wander about a bit, but after several mishaps in the past, they had promised to let their families know where they were when they explored, and of course, they hadn't mentioned this wee detour.

Ailsa operated the quad bike on the way back. She didn't rush, just meandered up the road, enjoying the beautiful fall weather. Although fall mornings could be quite chilly, the days would warm as the sun burned off the early morning mist.

The kids whizzed past on their quad bike. Tibbetts waited until he could no longer see or hear them, before he approached the lighthouse. He stopped and listened at the door. His tender feet felt sore on the course doormat. He looked down, and read these words, "Welcome to Mystic Island." *Could he assume he was on Mystic Island in Scotland?*

He didn't hear a sound, so he gently pushed the door open. A wooden sign on the door rattled as he pushed. He hurriedly held it still and read the words, "Mermaids Welcome, Sorry No Trolls." He chuckled, at least these people had a sense of humor! He stuck his head in and peered around. Something smelled amazing! In a flash he dashed across the room, his bare feet silent on the tile as he snatched the loaded platter and mug of tea off the counter. He drank the tea down in big gulps as he rushed outside.

As fast as his legs would carry him, he scrambled to his hiding place. Someone might return any minute! He had heard the girl call out, letting him know the breakfast was there.

Tibbetts had never tasted anything so good in his life! He tried not to devour it too quickly, but he was so hungry that the mound of food disappeared in seconds! He gulped in the last of it, then hid the cup and platter in the rocks. He felt a twinge of guilt while eating the food. “I’ll pay ‘im back,” he promised as he whispered the words out loud. “If I get a chance to do the right thing, I’ll definitely pay ‘im back!”

After the kids were long gone, Tibbetts nodded off.

CHAPTER 3

THE CASE OF THE MISSING TOWELS

The kids sped past the lighthouse toward the castle. Lessons awaited the kids back at the castle, but Ailsa thought it was just too nice to be cooped up indoors. She had a plan.

Fall holiday was almost upon them and there were many guests staying in the castle, which served the island as a lodge and restaurant. Socorro's family owned and operated the business and due to the holidays ahead, the place was buzzing with activity.

The island had become a source of rest and relaxation for many who enjoyed nature and wildlife. Photographers, fisherman, as well as tourists of all sorts, enjoyed staying in the historical castle and touring the scenic island. Scuba diving and golfing were also much desired sports in season.

Because their parents were so busy taking care of all the guests, it meant the kids were allowed to be independent. They made the most of it by planning in adventures, and sometimes even misadventures. They were known for that!

"Maybe we can take our lessons in the garden today; let's convince them to let us study outdoors!" she shouted over the sound of the engine.

There were not many students on the tiny remote Island where they lived. Home schooling was the only option for them. The kids were assigned lessons on Monday via email and a tutor arrived once a week on

Friday to check their progress and answer questions. The tutor assigned to them was stern, and they knew they'd better be on track when she arrived!

They usually studied in the library, to prevent distractions. The castle library was just what you'd expect, massive and filled with many old books! The floor to ceiling bookcases housed volumes from days gone by and if there were any newer books, they were all about island life. They found the most interesting thing in the room was the ladder, and they used it many times just to climb its steps to the top. They had a secret hope that in the books on the top shelves, they'd find some sort of treasure, like money hidden between pages, but so far, nothing of interest was found.

Socorro had the knack of convincing his mom that exploring for flora and fauna was better than sitting in a stuffy library. He'd much rather gather leaves outdoors to identify later, than sit about soaking up meaningless facts read on his tablet.

Ailsa was a much better student than her male pal and she consumed words like he consumed his breakfast. But she too, sought to finish as soon as possible each day. If she happened to finish everything by lunch, her mum allowed her to help in the kitchen. Cooking and baking were some of the many things she loved to do. She had a knack for it too, as she learned from her mum how to make tasty and nutritious meals. And Socorro loved to eat it all, never at a loss for appetite. His high energy, six-foot frame was pretty much bottomless.

Arriving back at the castle, the kids parked the four-wheeler in the garage. Entering through the back kitchen door, they found their moms in the kitchen. Adara, Socorro's mom, was studying the week's menus and writing down the groceries to be ordered. Mary, Ailsa's mum, was busy chopping veggies for the noon meal. She was the head chef of the castle and could usually be found in the kitchen.

It didn't take long for the kids to convince the busy ladies that studying in the garden would be a good idea. They agreed that fresh air and sunshine helped the mind and soul. "As long as yous stay on task," Mary cautioned. "And no wonderin' aboot."

Having acquired permission to study in the garden, they quickly gathered their books and electronic tablets and headed out. Foster, the Frazier family dog, joined them. She was an energetic golden retriever mix and a new mum of eight pups. She, too, was always up for an adventure. Usually, they would take her out on a leash to prevent her from wandering, but today, unbeknownst to the kids, she sneaked out behind them.

The garden was well kept and had plenty of benches, as well as grassy areas, for the kids to spread out on and study. Most of the beautiful summer flowers had faded, but with fall upon them, the reds and oranges of the changing leaves were a feast for their eyes.

Socorro flopped down on some fallen leaves near the little brook that flowed through the garden. He propped his tablet on a flat stone under one of the many statues that oversaw the workings of the garden. Ailsa sat down on a nearby bench and was just getting things set when Foster made her presence known as she began to bark. Then off she went, chasing something!

"Ach! There she goes again! She'd better not be after the ponies, or I'll tie a rope on her myself!" Ailsa called out.

Foster had a habit of chasing anything that moved and the wild Shetland ponies that ran free on the island were no exception. Her reputation for being a pest had even reached the cows that the kids had befriended. The "beasties" on the island had been put on alert to watch out for the dog. She was harmless but still a pest to the peace-loving animals.

Socorro pushed up from his leafy seat, but the area was moist (it rains almost daily in Scotland) and he had trouble getting traction. He slid around; swinging his arms about like windmill blades as he tried to stay upright. Unfortunately, he fell flat on his stomach.

"Ugh!" he cried out, his breath knocked out of him.

Ailsa couldn't help but laugh! Feeling a wee bit guilty, she got up from the bench and held her hand out to him.

"Wait a sec," he puffed, trying to catch his breath. He rolled onto his side and finally sat up. He grabbed Ailsa's hand as she dug her feet into the ground to brace herself and pull him up. But her tiny frame was no match for his bulk, and he fell back on his bottom.

"Socorro, stop messin' aboot! We'll neva catch Foster at this rate! She'll be long gone, in fact I cannae hear her barks noo!"

Socorro glared at her. He wasn't messing around! It was all a big accident! He held his tongue, though, as he examined the damage to his shoes and clothes. At this point, there wasn't a clean spot on them. He got up and stomped his feet, trying to rid himself of the thick, gooey mud.

"I'd better go in and change out of these wet clothes and ask permission to look for her. You know we'll be in for it if we just take off! I'm already doing extra chores from the last time we got in deep trouble with the folks."

Ailsa shook her head in frustration, as she gathered their school equipment. Socorro grabbed his tablet and they headed in. Now they would be behind in their studies!

Trouble likes to follow me around, Socorro thought. (And he wasn't wrong!)

The kids entered through the back due to the mud that Socorro was wearing. He took off his shoes and carried them as he hurried in.

"Wha's goin' on noo?" Ailsa's mum exclaimed. "You'd best get upstairs and ou' of those clothes before your mum sees ya!" she scolded Socorro.

Ailsa explained what happened and how Foster had run off while they were in the garden. "We need to find her, please, Mum." she begged.

"Well, let her come home on her own, then. That dawg is jist doin' what comes natural to 'er. She's a mum and she'll be back soon to care for the pups."

"But we should find 'er before she chases the ponies or other beasties!" Ailsa argued.

"No, Ailsa, donnae get stressed ou'! That dawg will come back on 'er own, for sure. Yous know what you need to be aboot. Noo get up to the library and get your work done, lass!" Mary turned her back to Ailsa and continued to knead the bread she was preparing. It was clear, the conversation was over.

~

Tibbetts wasn't sure how long he slept but he jerked awake when he heard a bark. A large yellow dog was headed straight for him! He hopped up and skedaddled for the sea! He dove into the frigid bay and disappeared in the water to hide himself from the dog! He was sure its incessant barking was going to bring the entire island down on him. But luckily, no one was about. Tibbetts watched as the golden retriever turned and entered the lighthouse.

Did I leave the door open? He was in such a hurry; he must have done.

As soon as the dog disappeared, he hurried out of the water. Shaking violently and chilled to the bone, he felt miserable! He needed to get warm quickly or risk hypothermia. He sneezed. Yikes! *I hope no one in the lighthouse heard that!* He trotted back to his hiding place.

~

Meanwhile, Gee made his way down the stairs to get his breakfast before the tea was cold. *I wonder wha' they brought me this mornin'*? But when he got there, the counter was empty! He gasped! No breakfast, just a muddy dawg! Gee frowned. Wha's goin' on? He glared at Foster. She wagged her tail, in slow motion and ducked her head a bit sheepishly. *Maybe the dog ate my food! But did she eat the plate too*? He'd heard Ailsa call out that it was ready, but where was it? He saw the thermos and poured himself a cup of tea. But the liquid in the thermos only filled the cup halfway up. He shook his head. He fished out a couple of protein bars from the cupboard. He'd have to make do with this since the kids seemed to have forgotten his breakfast!

The phone was ringing in the office when Socorro came back downstairs after changing his clothes. He was looking for Ailsa, or his dad. Foster was on the loose and he needed to find her! But no one was around. He answered the phone. "Castle Rossmore Lodging." Socorro held the receiver away from his ear. Gee was shouting and his eardrum recoiled from the noxious sound.

"Your dawg is here at the lighthouse, and she is a muddy mess! She has slung mud everywhere in this place and noo someone needs to come get her and clean it up! I think yous know who I mean! Where is my breakfast? All's tha' was left was a half-filled thermos of tea." He hung up and none too softly.

Well, could this day get any worse? And it was Friday. Kristal, his older sister, and Hamish, Gee's grandson, would be expected home from the university tonight. He needed to be finished with his studies and chores before then. *But what was Gee saying about his breakfast?*

I need ta find shelter and get off this beach, away from the lighthouse! Tibbetts told himself, building up the courage to move. He ran across the field toward the castle. He crouched down in the tall grass and hoped that no one could see him. The dog was in the lighthouse, and it seemed quiet at the castle. But how was he going to get in, in broad daylight?

He heard the engine of the quad bike again. Startled, he pressed himself to the ground. The boy was riding by with the dog loping along beside him on a rope. Yikes! If the dog caught his scent, there would be trouble. But they passed by without incident. He released his breath and thanked his lucky stars! As soon as they were far enough ahead that he wouldn't be detected, he trotted after them. Winded and weak, he finally made it to the garden behind the castle. He fell down on the grass and began to cough uncontrollably.

Ailsa was sitting near the open window of the library, studying. Since Socorro had ruined their study time in the garden, she decided to sit by the window to get some fresh air. She hadn't a clue where Socorro had got off to, until she saw him dismount the quad bike. It sounded like he was coughing his head off!

Socorro was leading Foster into the garden to hose her off. She was indeed covered with mud and would not be allowed indoors. But he needed dry towels. As cold as it was this morning, she would be chilled to the bone if he didn't dry her immediately.

He tied her rope to the nearest tree, then entered the castle via the garden door. Tibbetts, who had quickly stifled his cough, continued to watch the boy carefully from his hiding place.

Soon Socorro returned to the muddy dog, his arms loaded up with towels. She wagged her tail and pulled her ears back, smiling at him apologetically. He gave her a stern look and commanded her to sit. All he needed now was for her to jump on him with her muddy paws!

"Oh, man! I forgot the soap!" he shouted in frustration. He tossed the towels on a bench and scurried back into the castle.

This must be my lucky day! Tibbetts thought as he snatched the towels off the bench. The dog, tied on the short rope, set to barking and growling. But Tibbetts was long gone by the time the boy returned. Socorro unwound the hose in preparation to wash the dog. He reached back for a towel, but they were gone!

"Hey! Where's the towels?" he screeched! He looked at Foster. She wagged her tail. She was still tied snugly just as he left her, and no towels were lying about!

"I bet Ailsa is pranking me!" He threw up his hands in frustration and jogged back inside. There were guests in the house, so he snuck in quietly and ascended the stairs to the library.

Ailsa was sitting near the window, her nose in a book. *Yeah, look at her all innocent-like!* "You can't fool me, girl! Where are the towels?"

"Wha'? Are you plumb frembly?" (she was using puffin language meaning 'hard to get along with').

"Me! I know you're pranking me. The towels. You took the towels I was going to use on Foster."

"Socorro, I've been here, studyin' like ya should be! How'd you lose towels?" She stood up and placed her hands on her hips.

It wasn't like her to not own up to a prank. Usually, she'd be rolling on the floor laughing by now.

"You mean you didn't take them, for real?"

"For real. I've been right here. I pinky swear it!" she said, holding up her pinky.

"Well, if you didn't take them, where did they go?" he shrugged. Frustrated and tired, he went to hunt down more towels.

Weirdest day ever! he thought.

CHAPTER 4

DRY CLOTHES

Tibbetts shrugged off his drenched outer clothes and spread them in the sun to dry. He wrapped up in one of the large towels and used another to dry his wet hair. Getting out of the wet clothes provided him with some relief, but now he was half-naked.

What if someone finds me like this? he thought. *Do I dare go into the castle in this state?*

A large shiver came over him which left him little choice. So, without any more thought, he decided to sneak into the castle through the back garden door.

Once inside, he let his eyes adjust to the light. Surprisingly, no one was in sight. He quietly tiptoed down the long hall, tightly grasping the towel about his body. When he reached the end, he found himself at the entrance of a large dining area that was buzzing with guests! More food than he had ever seen in his entire life was spread over the enormous dining table. A wonderful aroma sent Tibbett's stomach into spasms, causing it to growl so loudly he was afraid it would blow his cover!

Hunkering down near the hall opening he began to ponder about what he should do next.

Thunk...thunk...thunk...

He heard a series of loud footsteps indicating someone was coming his way!

Frightened to be discovered, he jerked up and pressed himself as flat as he could against the cold, stone wall. *Clunk!* Suddenly the wall gave away, and he fell back! As he hit the ground, he bit his lip to keep from crying out!

The wall closed as quickly as it had opened, and he found himself in total darkness! Taking a moment to figure out what was going on, he was thankful that he hadn't been injured. However, he felt a chilled breeze and he realized he had lost his towel.

Ach! I cannae be found like this! he exclaimed to himself. *What a predicament.* But what could he do in total darkness without a source of light?

In nothing but his underwear he stood up and felt around for a light switch or a way out. But he only found shelves with what felt like cans and food packages on them. He must be in the room where the nonperishable food was stored! *Yay!* He was starving. Food at last. But what sort of food did he find? Carefully feeling each package, he settled on one that contained something squishy. He tore open the bag with his teeth. He sniffed the contents and stuck his hand inside. *Flumps*! (sweet, twisted marshmallow treats), one of his favorites. He devoured a handful, then folded the package top down to save the rest for later. Feeling around, he found a canvass sack full of potatoes. He poured them out onto the floor, so he could use the sack to gather more food. He put the *Flumps* in the bag and was able to snag some apples and bags of crisps, which he added. But much to his surprise, he spotted something that caused his heart to freeze inside him! Over in the corner, just out of arms reach, he saw two red glowing eyes! They seemed to be coming closer and closer, until he could feel heat of the creature's breath near his face and he cried out! "AHHHHH!"

Still clutching the bag, he jumped back from the thing and right onto the pile of potatoes! He slid about, doing his best not to fall over the rolling veggies.

Moments later, the door swung open. Light began to pour into the room, and he dove behind the nearest shelf. He was still breathing heavily from his recent fright. He looked around for the eyes, but they were gone.

Click.

Someone had activated the light! *Oh no, I'm a goner for sure,* he thought.

He pressed himself flat against the wall, holding his breath. From his hiding place, he was able to see an overweight lady in an apron rummaging through the pantry. While she was bent over, looking through a lower shelf, he rushed out the open door and found himself in the kitchen! Luckily, no one else was around. He began to look for a new hiding place and found an open door that led into a broom closet. Without any more thought, he leapt inside.

Brooms, mops, and buckets littered the floor haphazardly. He glanced around for anything he could use to cover himself with. On the back of the door hung an old apron. Lacking any other choice, he donned the apron. *This 'ill have to do. At least it covers up me underpants,* he blushed.

He turned a bucket over and sat down to think. *What does a lad in a frilly apron, hiding in a closet, do next?*

Realizing he still had the bag of food in his hand, he thanked his lucky stars and began to eat his fill.

"I'll repay them for this food, at some point," he said aloud, his mouth full. "If I'm nae sent straight back to Liverpool, or worse, that is!"

He shook his head. And speaking of head, he spotted a knit cap abandoned in the corner. He pulled it down over his damp locks. *Good choice! I already feel warmer.* A pair of wellie boots leaned against the wall, and he put those on his sore bare feet. *Wha' a sight I must be! A half-drowned lad in a lass's apron, knit camp and wellies!* He chuckled.

~

The family was gathering for supper, glad to welcome Gee's grandson, Hamish, and Socorro's older sister, Kristal, home from Uni for the weekend. Kristal was 16, and Hamish almost 19. They had just started their college studies in the fall. Hamish hadn't planned on going to the University in Edinburgh. He was content to stay on the island and learn from his granddad what it takes to run the lighthouse. But after a year's training by Gee, he realized that he needed more education. Learning how to interpret weather patterns would be such an asset for the islanders; he could keep them informed of severe weather. So, he enrolled in meteorology. And what a great choice it was, too. He loved it!

Since he was gone weekdays attending classes, Gee was on his own to keep the lighthouse running. So, Hamish relieved Gee on the weekends, so he could get the rest he needed. The sea took no holiday and must be monitored seven days a week! It was a busy schedule, for sure.

Kristal had finished her undergrad education early, and was studying interior design, photography and art. Her skills would be needed as the family further expanded the castle's capacity to house guests. There were many rooms yet to be updated from the majestic old castle decor, to new modern lodging.

She was also accomplished in archery. So much so that they hired her to teach classes at the Uni. It kept her skills up and she was able to compete for fun.

The conversation this evening revolved around the missing breakfast! Ailsa and Socorro retold how they left the breakfast for Gee, as usual. "Aye,

I placed the food on a platter, poured the tea and fixed it like Gee likes it. Plenty of cream and a wee taste of sugar! Then we left."

"Then why was there only the thermos on the counter when I came down, with jist a wee bit of tea left?" Gee asked.

"Well, someone must have taken the food!" Hamish said, "But who?"

"If it was jist the food gone, I'd say Foster ate it since she showed up looking hungry! And a muddy mess she was, too! But the platter and the cup, too? I donnae believe she could have eaten those!"

Everyone chuckled. It was a mystery for sure. But with no answers the conversation soon changed to other topics.

Fridays were always hectic. The ferry brought the weekend staff and the Uni students to the castle and then the weekday staff and departing guests went back to the city.

Tibbetts took advantage of the chaos. While everyone was busy elsewhere, he left his hiding place donned in his weird garb. He waited for a chance to sneak some supper. When no one was looking he quickly grabbed a few sandwiches.

The lad he'd been watching, headed upstairs. He stealthily followed him up, staying just out of sight. He watched as he traveled about halfway down the hall, then turned and entered a room. He waited patiently, hoping he wouldn't stay long in the room. After a short while, the lad came out and got into the elevator.

Rory waited to make sure the floor was vacant, then slinked down the hall and into the boy's room. And what a room it was!!

There was a fireplace along one wall that heated the massive room. He backed up close to it to warm himself. It didn't provide much heat, though, since the embers were almost out. He stood there a minute to scope the place out. A grand bed, unlike anything he'd ever seen before, sat beneath a window. The bed clothes were a bit mussed, like they were spread up quickly. The lad must do his own cleaning!

The rest of the furniture was heavy and of the fine quality you'd expect in a castle. He noticed a wardrobe in the corner. It was full of clothing and shoes, which he could easily see since the door had been left open. He walked over and took out a few and discovered they were all close to his own size! Feeling braver than he should have, he headed to the bathroom for a shower.

The hot water was heavenly, and the best part was, he finally felt warm! He could have stayed in there all day, but he cut it short so he wouldn't be discovered. He dried off with a couple of thick, warm towels. Then he tried on a pair of the lad's jeans. He'd have to roll up the legs of the trousers a bit, but that was no problem. At least they were dry and much better than the frilly apron! He "borrowed" a shirt and jumper as well. He took off the wellies and put on a pair of socks and shoes. Almost perfect size! He stuffed the apron and wet towels under a few logs in the fireplace. But what should he do with the wellies? He went over and opened the window and tossed them out! He watched as they hit the ground below and bounced into some shrubbery. Done!

He then slipped out the same way he came in. Voila! He had survived the sea, the cold—and, at least for today, detection!

Now to find a place to hide for the night.

CHAPTER 5

THE DRONE

It was a chilly Saturday morning, but Socorro didn't mind. He was enjoying a bit of solitude as he fed the baby-doll sheep. He enjoyed petting the soft, fluffy animals, even when they butt and pushed at him.

These adorable little creatures were small enough to pick up and carry around, if you wanted to. And today, he wanted to. He snuggled with the weest one, Flumpy. He enjoyed her soft baa next to his ear. Her jagged breath tickled his ears and made him laugh! But the moment was short lived because she was a wiggly one, forcing him to set her down to prevent her from falling.

Caring for the sheep was just one of his chores. He also cared for the birds and wild animals on the island. It was a job he loved but one where he couldn't let his guard down. Evil lurked at every turn, even out here on this remote island. He'd learned that being secluded from people didn't seclude you from evil forces, because they exist everywhere. He'd learned that on *Mystic Mountain!*

There were many creatures depending on he and Ailsa. Besides the snowy owl that was on the brink of extinction, the peregrine falcons nested here. They, too, were on the endangered list and attracted many guests who loved to view and photograph them. Artists also loved to paint the magnificent creatures, and they had their share of them here on the island. But there were also poachers about, looking to steal eggs or capture the birds themselves. They would bring in big money when sold on the black market. Their access to the sea made them vulnerable to them.

Because of the many places poachers could access the island, Socorro found he could watch the birds better with a drone. He was proud of the fact he had worked hard and got his drone license.

He had become proficient in piloting it close enough to the nests and roosting areas to watch them carefully. The model he purchased was equipped with a quiet motor, perfect for taking pictures without disturbing the nests. He could quietly photograph the activities of the birds, and he logged them on his computer to keep track of all the eggs, and the exact number in each nest. An added benefit was the wide-angle view that helped him keep an eye out for poachers.

Later today, he planned to fly his drone around the cliffs, the beach and other nesting areas. He would wait until dusk, when certain birds were more active, such as the owls.

But for now, he must finish his chores. He paused. Was someone watching him? He looked up and saw his grandmother waving at him from her window. Whew, just Grammy. He sighed and waved back as she signaled for him to come. Her urgent signal caused him to quit what he was doing and hurry up to her room.

"Hi, Grammy! How are all the pups?" Socorro asked as he entered his Grandparent's living area.

"Hi, Socorro, the pups are fine, growing like weeds! But Foster keeps asking to go out. I guess it's time to take her for her morning walk."

"Okay." Socorro replied. It was another of his responsibilities.

"I bet Foster will be weaning these pups soon. I think she's looking forward to getting her independence back." Pop said.

"And although I'm a bit sad about them leaving us, I'm glad too! Eight youngin's are a lot of work!"

Grammy chuckled.

Socorro scooped up the closet pup and let it lick his cheeks. "Oh, aren't you a cutie!" he cooed.

The pup wiggled and licked until Socorro burst out laughing. He set it back in the dog bed next to its siblings.

"Dad told me that the lady up the road already picked one out to take home. I bet they all go fast, who can resist a puppy? I wish we could keep a few of them, though."

"Don't you have enough animals to care for?" Pop asked.

"Yeah, you're probably right. Foster is a handful. But she'll always be number one in my book!" Foster looked up at him and wagged her tail. Socorro attached the leash to her collar and patted her head. She pulled him toward the door.

"Bye!" he called as he rushed out behind the anxious dog.

Last night, as a fugitive in the castle, Tibbetts had sneaked around and found an abandoned room on the top floor, hidden away near the turret. An old, bare, mattress laid over in a corner. He stretched his tired form on it. It wasn't bad, better than lots of places he'd slept in recently. It was warm and dry and softer than the floor. Before he knew it, he was asleep.

This morning, he awoke to the sun rays from the bare window. He sat up, trying to remember where he was. *Oh, yeah, I'm in the castle!*

His stomach growled loud enough to wake the dead! He remembered he had the sack of food he'd found the day before. He rummaged around and pulled out an apple. Afterwards, being extremely bored, he tiptoed down the hall and "borrowed" a book from the library. There were so many in there, he figured no one would miss one. Besides, he planned to return it when he finished. He made a note of the place he took it from.

He sneaked down to the garden, the book under his arm.

He propped up against a tree trunk. He had come down early this morning and found his old clothes that were spread out to dry. He grabbed them up quickly and hid them under a rock. No one had seen them, he guessed, since they were lying just as he left them in the garden. Silly of him to forget them! An all-out search could ensue if they were found! Then...well, he'd be in trouble.

The book was an exciting story about pirates and treasure chests, and he'd become so engrossed in it he'd let the boy sneak up. Now the dog was barking.

"Hey, who's there?" Socorro cried out. Tibbetts held his breath. He was well hidden behind the tree trunk unless they came further.

Not seeing anyone and not getting a reply, Socorro shrugged and walked on. Foster was still on alert, but he figured she smelled a squirrel or something. Foster strained on her leash and was acting crazy as they approached the next tree. Maybe he'd better walk her somewhere besides the garden, too many squirrels had her in fits. Besides, they both needed new scenery. So, he tugged her back and wandered out of the garden and on down the path. Tibbetts sighed in relief! *That was too close for comfort!*

Soon, Socorro found himself in the village. The two of them scurried into one of the buildings open this time of the morning on a Saturday.

"Gud mornin', Socorro," Danny, the proprietor of the fishing shop said. "How can I help yous, today?"

They made their way to the counter. Foster wagged her tail and smiled at the kind man. She was hoping for a treat and she wasn't disappointed! Danny reached behind the counter and supplied her with her favorite, and a pat on the head.

"We're just stoppin' in to say hi and to find out when the next fishing excursion is." he said.

"Aye, we have one booked for Sunday!" Danny knew Socorro's love for fishing, and they had this conversation frequently.

Socorro's face dropped. He couldn't go on Sunday. He was involved in all the devotional services held at the castle.

"I'll have to miss that one, I guess. But thanks. I'll check back later and see if there's more scheduled for next week." He headed for the door. "And Foster says thanks for the treat!" Socorro waved and they left as Foster wagged her tail, happily.

"We'd better be getting back, girl. If were gone too long, Mom and Dad will be worried. And if we make them worry, there will be dire consequences to pay!" he said to the dog. She pulled her ears back in agreement as they turned toward home. Her hungry puppies were waiting.

Tibbetts peeked out from the trash bin he had chosen to hide behind. *Where did that lad go*? Then he caught sight of him walking his dog briskly away from the castle. He stealthily followed, keeping far enough behind to not alarm the dog. He'd like to make friends with the teen, whom he gauged to be about his age, and maybe even solicit his help. He could tell him the dilemma he was in. But just when he thought he had enough courage to do so, he'd panic! Hiding was safe. The only problem was he was so lonely!

He'd been on his own since his dad's passing. On his own and alone, with no one to talk to! He was a social type and really needed human contact. But here he was again, alone on this sparsely populated island. He swiped at his eyes and swallowed hard. He'd better get out of this mindset, or he'd run out begging for help!

He followed as close as he could, hopping from one hiding spot to another all the way into the wee village and back. He breathed a sigh of relief that he hadn't been discovered, but what a wasted trip! Nothing much to see in the village and he was still no closer to getting to know the lad.

He hid near the garage as the boy and dog entered the castle through the back entrance. Suddenly, he heard a raucous and saw the sheep running about, bleating loudly. *Wha's goin' on?*

He could see movement in the tall grass, but not whatever was there. A creepy feeling came over him. Was it snakes, or other scary beasties? Something had the sheep in a tizzy. He needed to move before anyone came out to check on the noise! But where could he go to hide? He trotted back to the garden. It had the most hiding places near the castle.

~

Socorro somehow made it through the long day. He missed Ailsa when she was gone on the weekends. Hamish was at the lighthouse helping Gee, and Kristal was hanging out with Mom, chatting about her week. Socorro had been left to find his own entertainment.

Maybe he could get his sister to help him with the drone later, since Hamish was at the lighthouse. Kristal always perked up when she had a chance to be with the handsome Scottish bloke! It was better to send the drone out just before all the daylight was gone. So, he waited until that evening.

He retrieved his drone from his closet shelf. His and Kristal's rooms were next door to each other and were joined by a Jack and Jill bathroom, (they shared a bathroom between the rooms and could walk from one to the other's room through the bath area).

The rooms had been picked out for them when they first moved in, by the kind caretaker. They were fancily embellished and yet suited their needs, so they had settled in there. Their parents' room was just across the hall, and their grandparents' suite just beyond that, so the family was all together on the same wing. It helped with communication and the running of the lodging business.

The castle was equipped with 35 bedrooms, so there were plenty of options, had they wanted something different. But Socorro felt his room suited him fine. And apparently Kristal felt the same way since she had never moved. Kristal found her own bathroom down the hall, though. She told Socorro he was too messy, and she didn't want to share one with him!

Socorro went through the bath area and knocked on Kristal's door.

"Yea, what's up?" she said, as she appeared at the door. "You can come in." A fire was blazing in the fireplace, pushing back the chill. The fire and a few flickering candles provided the only light in the room. The fruity aroma of the candles made him want something to eat. "Hey, what's that smell. It makes me want to grab an orange, or grapefruit!"

Kristal grinned. "Yes, my candles are citrus scented. And no, you can't have a bite of one!" They laughed.

"I'm going out to check on the birds. Do you want to come with me? If we hurry, we can make it back before supper. It'll just be a quick check since I've almost waited too late" Socorro said, glancing at his watch.

"Sure, I'll come. But you're right, we need to hurry!" Kristal flipped the switch to turn on the overhead light and glanced at herself in the mirror.

Socorro rolled his eyes. "Hurry, Sis. You look fine. I'm sure Hamish thinks you're pretty no matter what!"

Kristal punched him on the bicep. "Stop with the teasing, and hand me my sweatshirt off the chair!"

Socorro grinned, as he tossed her the shirt. Teasing Kristal was his favorite past time, next to teasing Ailsa!

They asked for a ride to the lighthouse. It was less than a mile from the castle. But in the evenings, the temperature dropped drastically.

Pop said he would take them since he wanted to talk to Gee, anyway. Kristal didn't have a license to drive yet. In Scotland, a driving license can't be obtained until you're at least eighteen.

Pop pulled up close to the lighthouse and cut the engine. He and Kristal went in while Socorro set up the drone. It was equipped with bright lights so he could still use it at night. He could even do some photography, although the pictures would turn out grainy and harder to see.

The busy group had no idea there was a stowaway in the back of the pick-up. Tibbetts saw that there were large tarps in the back of the truck, so he slid under them. Might as well see where everyone was headed.

Socorro started the drone and used his remote to guide the device. He searched the area, looking for the nesting birds. The whir of the small engine made Tibbetts shake! A drone? How could he sneak out and see what was going on if the lad had a drone? He held his breath and froze in place. *Whirr, whirr,* it sounded like it was just above him. He froze until he couldn't hear the drone any longer, then slowly eased out from under the cover. He hopped over the fenders and hit the ground. *Crunch!* His feet hitting the ground made quite a noise! He gulped and hunkered down near the truck. Maybe the lad hadn't heard!

CHAPTER 6

WHERE THERE'S SMOKE

Socorro was engrossed trying to make out what he could on the grainy view finder. He maneuvered the remote, guiding the drone back. *What was that?* He heard a noise by the truck. He pulled the drone in and snuck back to the pickup, just as Tibbetts decided to get back in, to prevent discovery. But it was too late! He nearly collided with the lad!

"Hey, who are you?" Socorro called out as Tibbetts turned to run. Socorro ran behind him and with his long legs caught up to him in no time. He grabbed his hood and pulled him back. They both landed on the ground.

"Watch out! You almost made me drop my drone! Those things are expensive, Dude!" Socorro cried, scowling. He moved the drone from under his arm to the ground. They sat there looking at each other in the dim light.

Tibbetts talked rapidly, his heart racing. "Wait! I can explain! I'm lost. I fell from a boat and washed up here, near the lighthouse! I'm not lyin'."

Socorro stared at the boy with the thick British accent. His hair was mussed, and he was thin, his face drawn. Then he noticed the sweatshirt he had on. He had one just like it! And the pants! He had some like those too. *Wait! He has on my clothes!* He knew they were his because they were athletic wear and had his school mascot on the leg. "I'm not sure I can believe ya! Those are my clothes you have on, and yeah, those are my shoes, too! How did you get my clothes?"

Kristal and Hamish appeared, trying to see what all the shouting was about. The boys were still on the ground, so they reached down and helped them up. Everyone stared at Tibbetts.

"Let's get inside before we freeze to death and figure out who this guy is! He just showed up here and he has on my clothes, which by the way, are stolen!" Socorro shouted.

"Borrowed!" Tibbetts yelled back.

The group gathered by the fire. Pop and Gee joined them.

"First things first, can you tell us what brought you to the island?" Gee asked.

"Wait," Pop chimed in, "maybe we should start with introductions. I'm Pop to my grand-kids here. This is Socorro, and this is Kristal, my son's two kids." —Pop paused and turned— "This is Hamish, he lives here at the lighthouse with his grandfather."

"Everyone calls me Gee. Now what's your name?"

Tibbetts had to think fast. He decided to make up a name, for now. "I'm Orcher Billingham. I can explain wha' happened if yous jus' give me a chance! I've nawt been 'ere long, but I didnae steal from ya! I had to borrow because I was soaked and freezin'! If yous will take me back to the 'ouse, I'm sure I can explain." He shivered and wrapped his arms around his chest. He looked around at the group of kids and elderly men. He figured if he kept talking, they might just feel sorry enough for him to help him out.

"To be honest, I'm cold and 'ungry. Any chance I could get warmed up and beg a meal?" he pleaded.

Kristal spoke up, "Sure, let's all go back to the house. It's time for supper. We'll eat and then there will be plenty of time to figure it all out."

~

"Great, just in time," Mom called, as the group filed in. "The meal is served."

They gathered around the massive dining table. The staff numbers had grown so large that the family had to move from their usual place in the kitchen to the dining table, which was once reserved for guests only.

Pop guided the lad forward. "Adara, we have another guest, could you please see that they set another place?" Then he turned to the other lanky lad in the room. "Socorro, take him to your room and let him wash up before dinner. But hurry, we're already behind schedule."

Socorro frowned. He didn't like this new kid. Something about him wasn't right. And the fact he stole his clothes set him askew. He'd been in his room alone, going through his stuff. But he tried not to be rude.

"Come on," he said, already leaving the room.

When Socorro opened the door to his room, a thick cloud of smoke poured out into the hall, causing the fire alarms to sound! "Yikes! Fire!" Socorro waved his arms to dispel the smoke. Once the air cleared a bit, he didn't see any flames. He covered his nose with his shirt tail and peered in. The fireplace was lit. The smoke was coming from there. *Maybe the flue was shut!* Socorro rushed in, Tibbetts behind him.

"We need to get the flue open, now!" Socorro said.

"Wait, It's nawt the flue! It's me wet clothes I hid. I though' they'd burn up but guess they were too wet!" Tibbetts exclaimed.

Sure enough, there were smoldering clothes in the fireplace! Socorro frowned, then glared!

Dad appeared just then, fire extinguisher in hand! "Out of here, boys, hit the stairs," he shouted! The alarms were still going off, but thankfully the smoke had dissipated some.

"Wait, Dad. Orcher says he stuffed some wet things in there and that's what's causing all the smoke. Dad set the extinguisher down and used the poker to fish out the wet clothes and towels and drag them onto the stone hearth. He then used the fire extinguisher to thoroughly soak them. When there was no sign of smoke, he turned to Socorro.

"Well, it looks like you're right. It's all out. Let's go tell the others it's safe to come back in. I made sure everyone evacuated safely before I started looking for the source. When I saw smoke escaping out the stairwell door, I knew it was on this level and that you boys had just come up! I think I just aged twenty years!" Dad ran his hands through his hair and sighed. "I'm just glad the sprinklers didn't go off and ruin everything!"

Socorro turned to see what Orcher had to say, but he was gone!! "Where's Orcher?" Socorro yelped.

"Well, I told you boys to get out. Hopefully he did as I asked. Where did you find the kid? What is he doing here? Any parents around?" Dad asked.

"We don't know yet. We were going to give him the third degree at supper, I mean ask him what he is about. But then before we even got washed up, the smoke poured out and the rest is history!"

"I'll get someone to come clean up this mess before you go to bed. I want to know why he would stuff wet things into the fireplace like that. And when?"

"All I know is he was snoopin' around down at the lighthouse. He tried to run off, but I caught him, and we both fell down as we struggled. That's when I noticed he had my clothes and shoes on! I guess he came up here and stole them, then stuffed his wet clothes in the fireplace."

Dad shook his head. "Sounds like he might be in some trouble. Let's go see if we can help him out, if we can find him again. Not likely he'll get too far, though. This Island is not that big."

"Well, there's thousands of places to hide in the castle alone, if he wants to. Guess we could get Foster to help us sniff him out!" Socorro said as they descended the stairs.

The two of them joined the others outside. When dad told them it was all clear, the group hurried in, since it was so frigid, and no one had time to grab their coats.

Dad made an announcement. "I'm so sorry for the inconvenience! It seems there was a slight problem with one of the fireplaces and smoke set off the alarms. There is no fire, and no one is in danger. Please return to what you were doing, and again, please accept my apologies."

There was a lot of mumbling and sour looks, but overall, no one complained too badly, at least not yet. Still Orcher was nowhere to be found.

"Please, sit down and eat a bite. I'm sorry if it's cold, we'll just have to make do tonight." Mom said.

"But where's the new kid?" Hamish inquired. He sat down in his usual spot and eyed the food hungrily.

"Well, he knows where the food is, hopefully he'll return to eat. If not, guess we'll be searching after supper." Mom answered.

They held hands and prayed as they always did before a meal. Pop prayed this time, and he thanked God for safety from the fire, for the family and food. He even prayed for the new boy, Orcher.

But where was he? Only God knew.

CHAPTER 7

FOUND

They spent so much time searching for the lost boy, the weekend flew by. But then, it always seemed to go by in a flash when the family was together. As much as Socorro hated to admit it, he missed Hamish and Kristal when they were gone. He and Kristal had become close during their time on *Mystic Mountain*. It seems to happen when you're lost and struggling for your life together. You can't go through that kind of adversity and not feel connected! And Hamish had helped them in so many endeavors this past year, he had become a good pal to Socorro and even something a bit more to his sister.

But, although they had looked everywhere, the kid eluded them. Much prayer had been offered up for that boy!

On a happier note, Ailsa and Mary would be back! Socorro looked forward to it, since Mary was the best cook! The weekend staff were good, but Mary had a gift. Her cinnamon buns were to die for!

And of course, Ailsa had become a good friend. Maybe even like a partner in crime. She loved to explore the castle and the moors as much as he did.

The Sunday night switchover was like the Friday one, in reverse! The ferry came in, the staff that worked during the week disembarked, and the Uni students and weekend staff got aboard, with a quick meal between. Then it was chaos while they all sped off to the docks. When the booming fog horns sounded, the ferry meant business. If you weren't aboard, you would be left behind.

Socorro took Ailsa's bag up to her room. It was directly across the hall from her mum's on the staff wing. Since Ailsa was prone to stay up late on her tablet, or reading, she needed her own space where she didn't bother her mum. Mary turned the lights out early, since she was responsible for having everything ready for breakfast each day. That required rising in the wee hours of the morning. Socorro and Ailsa didn't get up until just before breakfast at 7:30 each day, cherishing every wink of sleep.

He set the bag just outside the door for her. She would be up shortly. She was still saying her last goodbyes to Kristal. Instead of musical chairs, it was musical family.

Tibbetts watched from the upstairs window, being careful to stay out of view. The family was telling the college kids goodbye. He paced back and forth, trying to figure out what to do next! After the fireplace debacle, they were sure to kick him to the curb! He laid low all weekend, avoiding the family, but how long could he hide? This wasn't much of a life, hiding out, stealing food and being bored all day.

As Ailsa headed back in, she saw movement near an upstairs window. She looked up. Tibbetts jumped back, trying to stay out of sight. But it was probably too late!

Resigned to face his fate rather than spend any more time alone, he sat down in the middle of the room and waited. He was so tired! He was tired physically, but also tired of the loneliness and pain he faced each day. Someone would be up soon, and at this point, that was okay. If they sent him back, so be it. He'd make different choices this time, even though he had no clue what that would be!

When the lad and his younger counterpart burst into the room. Tibbetts actually felt relieved. This waiting game was over.

"We finally found ya!" Ailsa threw up her hands dramatically. "Socorro told me they looked for you all weekend. I donnae why you've been causing everyone so much trouble!"

"I weren't lookin' to cause trouble, was I?" Tibbetts scowled.

"We weren't sure if you were safe. Mom was worried about what you've had to eat and such." Socorro said, looking around the sparse room. Other than an old blanket, and a sheet-less mattress, the room was empty and cold. This was one of the rooms not yet remodeled.

"I know yous are mad at me?" Tibbetts said sheepishly. "I borrowed your clothes, helped me self to food and started a fire! I'm expectin' you'll throw me out to the wolves!"

Ailsa just stood there looking at him, her mouth wide open like she'd never seen a lad before! What she saw alarmed her. *He's all cut up and wounded!* She drew in a quick breath. His tattered and torn clothing exposed scraped and bleeding skin. His hair, dirty and matted, was clumped with dried blood. Both of his eyes were black and bruised, one swollen completely shut. His lips were swollen, and blood dripped from his nose! Without meaning to, she stepped back, appalled at his condition.

Socorro stared at her. She was being rude, staring and moving away. It wasn't like her at all. He ignored her weird behavior and answered the boy.

"Well, if you have good reasons why you did all this, then I'm sure Dad will understand. But you need to come and talk to my parents," Socorro said, "if you want help, that is."

The lad stared back at Ailsa. *Why is the lass acting so weird?* he thought. He wasn't that appalling, was he?

Socorro tried to soften the moment. "Hey, I don't think you've met Ailsa...Ailsa, this is uh, Vineyard, oops I think I forgot your name. What was it again?" Socorro looked back for Ailsa, but she was gone.

Tibbetts stood up. He was searchin' his memory. *What did I say my name was? I know I didnae say, Vineyard! Oh, yeah, Orcher!* He laughed! "I'm Orcher. And sorry, but I forgot your name, too."

While the boys were talking upstairs, Ailsa flew down to the kitchen. "Mum, we need help! The lad is hurt, bad! I think he has been beaten to pieces! He's in bits! Come on, be quick and bring the first-aid box."

Mary, busy preparing the baked goods for the next day, looked at her daughter, "Wha's wrong? Slow down and tell me wha' youre goin' on aboot. Wha' lad?" Mary asked, drying her hands on her apron.

"The lost one! Remember the lad we brought in? He's upstairs but he's in bad shape! Please hurry!"

Mary went to the pantry and grabbed the first-aid box. They rushed out, trotting as they ascended the back stairs, the quickest route. But they stopped abruptly because they nearly ran into the boys as they were descending. Mary quickly assessed both lads. They were fine, no bruises, no blood, nothing.

Ailsa blinked. *Is this the same lad I just saw?*

"Socorro, is this the lad that is hurt?" Mary inquired, as she wrinkled her brow.

Socorro stared at them, then shook his head. "Not that I know of." He looked at Ailsa, a puzzled look on his face. "Anyway, I was about to introduce you when you ran off. Orcher, this is Mary, she's our cook and Ailsa is her daughter."

Again, Ailsa stood there speechless. Where were the wounds she saw? Was she going daft?

Mary spoke up, "Ailsa thought you were needin' first aid. Guess you're okay, then?"

"I'm fine. I'm a wee bit hungry, but other than tha', there's no need for them bandages." Orcher nodded toward the box in her hand.

"Well, let's go down to the kitchen then, and I'll get ya something to eat." Mary said.

"Yeah, I'd like a snack, too." Socorro piped up.

Mary smiled and turned around as they all went to the kitchen.

While the boys were eating, Ailsa slinked into the sitting room and eased herself into one of the overstuffed chairs. *Why did the lad look so different upstairs*! She gulped and rested her head back, clearly shaken.

After the boys finished eating, they joined Ailsa. "Are you here for the devotional already? It's still an hour until it starts." Socorro said.

Ailsa gulped. She felt a wee bit lightheaded.

"You, okay? You look like you saw a ghost or something. Your mum would say you look peely wally." Socorro told her.

"Aye, I'm fine. A wee bit tired, I guess, from the weekend."

Orcher sat down near Ailsa. Socorro gave him a stern look, "Don't move!" he warned, then went in pursuit of his dad.

Tibbetts glanced around at his surroundings. He'd never seen anything like it before. Painted on the ceiling, there were a host of wee cherubs flying through puffy white clouds and blue skies. Thick gold-colored molding enhanced the elaborately embossed wallpaper. But that wasn't the only gold in the room. The stair railings were painted gold as well, perched on thin, white decorative spirals that lined the wide staircase. The cushions they sat on were woven with scarlet-colored thread, the identical color of the plush carpet on the stairs. It all dripped of money. *Posh* would be the English word for it!

A street orphan in a palace! He almost pinched himself. But there was no way these rich elites would take him in. *I'll be shipped out of here*. No use hoping he was going to get to stay! He gulped. *Where will I be sent?* He closed his eyes and took a deep breath. He had to think of something to tell them to let him stay here! *But what story can I invent, that will explain why I'm here without identification or passport?* He shook his head. He was in so much trouble! He sighed and stared at the floor. His face reflected on the shiny waxed surface and seemed to laugh at him. He felt the heat of anger rise in his chest. All he ever wanted was a home, stability and a steady food source. *Was that too much to ask?*

He wrapped his arms around his belly. His gut hurt. The food he had just eaten felt like a rock. *Please donnae send me back to Liverpool!* he pleaded, silently. He was so lost in his thoughts he jumped when Ailsa spoke.

"I'm sorry I was actin' so strangely, upstairs. I, uh, though' you were hurt. And in all the confusion I've forgotten your name."

"Why did ya think tha'? Me name is Orcher. I've been through some stuff, but I'm nae hurt."

"But I think you are. Not physically, like I first though', but deep down. On the inside, I mean. There's pain there that others cannae see. I saw it though, and it's the kind tha's worse than cuts and bruises." Ailsa couldn't believe she was saying this to Orcher. But she felt like she must. Like God had revealed it to her and she needed to help him.

Orcher scowled. "How would a wee girl know about such stuff? You're rich and live in this enormous castle." Orcher spread his hands out, gesturing to the room.

Ailsa swallowed and quickly answered. "Well, I'm nae rich and I donnae actually live here. I mean, I live here, but jist as a guest since my mum is the cook."

"But the lad you hang out with seems more like a pal than a boss. Am I right?"

"Aye, Socorro and I are pals. But I'm saying I'm nae rich. Not with money anyway. Guess it's complicated."

"Yeah. But still, you have no idea aboot what I've been through. Couldnae even guess!"

He looked away and scowled.

"You're right. I donnae know ya a 'tall. But I can see your pain."

"Again, how? I'm thinkin' it's time you minded your own business! Go and hang out with your rich pals." He crossed his arms and scowled.

Ailsa frowned as she pushed her strawberry curls away from her eyes and got up. She hurried into the kitchen.

I guess I overstepped my mark! But wait! God revealed the cuts and the wounds to me! Why? All she knew was that it was a bit scary and a lot weird! She shrugged.

I'll have to ask God what He wants me to do and say to Orcher, next. How can I reach him? His pain is causing him to shut others out. She sat down at the kitchen table and bowed her head in prayer. No time like the present to seek answers.

CHAPTER 8

CHANGED

Socorro found his dad in the business office going over the devotional for the evening. "Dad!" Socorro said a bit too loudly, as he burst through the door.

Kris, absorbed in what he was reading, jumped, "Socorro, no need to shout!" he said, somewhat perturbed at his impetuous son.

"Sorry, but you'll want to hear this! I found where the kid was hiding! He's in the sitting room with Ailsa. But guess where I found him?" Socorro paused, hoping his dad would throw out some guesses. "He was camping out in one of the vacant bedrooms, like a criminal. Why do you think he's been hiding?"

Kris scooted his rolling chair back from the desk and picked up his Bible. "Who knows? But right now, it's time for devotionals so all this will have to wait. We'll get to the bottom of it later. Let's go."

The family had been conducting nightly devotionals in the castle for several years now. Since the opening of Rossmore Castle Lodging, the island had gone from a sleepy village to a vibrant one, full of potential. But there wasn't a church on the island, so the devotionals in the castle helped fill the spiritual needs of the people. Many of the guests joined in when they heard the music start.

Socorro went back to the sitting area to find Ailsa and "Orcher." People were beginning to gather in the area, finding seats and getting ready for the devotional time. Some of them were standing around in groups, chatting as they waited for the service to start.

Tibbetts got up and found a place in the back of the room. He felt conspicuous where he had been sitting by the young lass, so the far corner in the back would suit him fine. Maybe he could get in a snooze, since he hadn't slept well in months.

Mary, Ailsa's mum, came from the kitchen and sat down on the bench in front of the grand piano. Without any introduction, she started to play. Her hands glided over the keys like a butterfly fluttering over a flower. Tibbetts leaned back in his chair, as he listened. The most beautiful melody filled the room. He sat up straighter. In spite of his desire to tune it all out, he was enthralled.

The small group of people took their seats as the music started. Ailsa came over and stood by her mum near the piano. She turned around to face the group. The room grew quiet. She closed her eyes and began to sing. She started out quietly, but her voice grew into one of the loveliest sounds Tibbetts had ever heard! His jaw dropped and he sat stone still.

The song was one familiar to him, *Amazing Grace*[1] . He remembered his mum singing it when he was a wee lad. He became so entranced he felt his heart start to melt. It was a feeling so indescribable that he was glad he was in the back because he felt a mist form in his eyes. All the emotions of the past few years welled up inside of him and he felt how broken he was. The loss of his parents and his stable home, the day to day danger of the city streets and the evil of the pirates overwhelmed him. He felt empty in other ways too, but he couldn't put his finger on what that was. He wiped his nose on his sleeve. *This could be embarrassing!* If he had been closer to the

1. Amazing Grace – John Newton

exit, he would have fled. But instead, he sat frozen to the chair as he listened while she sang all four verses:

Amazing grace! how sweet the sound,
That saved a wretch; like me!
I once was lost, but now am found,
Was blind, but now I see.

'Twas grace that taught my heart to
fear,
And grace my fears relieved;
How precious did that grace appear
The hour I first believed!

The Lord hath promised good to me,
His word my hope secures;
He will my shield and portion be
As long as life endures.

When we've been there ten thousand
years,
Bright shining as the sun,
We've no less days to sing God's praise
Than when we first begun.

As she finished, the unique sound of bag pipes filled the air. Gee entered the room playing the same tune, *Amazing Grace*, on the large instrument, not missing a note. The bagpipes rang out clear and strong in the high-ceiling room. The acoustics here were like that of a grand cathedral! Tibbetts felt the music seep deep into his soul...past the grief, over the wounds, and pound into the very ventricles of his heart.

The entire group stood to their feet and sang along. "Amazing Grace! How sweet the sound..."

Tibbetts began to sob. He was done for. He melted into a puddle then and there! He tried to pull in his emotions, but it was no use! He was a heap; a mound of hurt and pain dripping from every orifice! Ailsa was right! He was badly injured and now he was overcome with it. Wounded and bleeding from the very innermost part, he fell on his face before all these strangers.

Socorro's parents and many of the others came and laid their hands on him. Kris began to pray out loud.

"Our Father in heaven, we bless your Holy name. Lord, we thank you for all you've done and for all you're about to do. I know your spirit is here, we feel you." His voice rose in volume, "Father, heal this young man. Touch him and make him whole." Then Kris prayed with Tibbetts as he surrendered his heart to the One who heals.

After the prayer, Tibbetts felt a strange warmth enter his body. It started at the top of his head and even made his toes tingle.

He sat up. The rocks in his gut were gone! His broken heart felt joy! As God's Holy spirit worked on his heart, he opened himself to it. Tears poured down his face. Embarrassed by his show of emotion, he looked about. But no one was laughing at him, they were all smiling, some with tears in their own eyes.

He stood up. He raised his hands unashamedly and shouted, "I donnae know how, but God, you've healed me from the guilt, the pain, the hate!" He then quietly whispered, "Thank you!" The relief he felt was indescribable!

The group began to clap. They clapped and clapped and then they sang. Socorro made eye contact with him. He smiled and the anger that Tibbetts had once seen there, had softened.

Tibbetts had no clue what had happened to him, but he knew it was miraculous. All the things he always longed for seemed to fill his being. It was weird, but in a very good way!

After the song, Kris asked them to take their seats. He opened his Bible and read from Revelations:

"To the angel of the church in Laodicea write: These are the words of the Amen, the faithful and true witness, the ruler of God's creation. Here I am! I stand at the door and knock. If anyone hears my voice and opens the door, I will come in and eat with that person, and they with me." Revelations 3:14, 20

"I think Orcher just heard a knock on his heart's door. Is that right, Orcher?" Kris asked.

"Tha's right!" he paused. "And I must confess, I lied aboot me name! I'm not Orcher, I'm Tibbetts. Rory Tibbetts, but me friends just call me Tibbetts. And I have a story to tell ya, but it's a long one, so I'll save it for later."

Kris came over and patted him on the back in a friendly manner. Socorro offered a high-five and Ailsa just smiled at him.

Tibbetts addressed the young lass, "Ailsa, I want ta apologize. You were right. I was injured and broken. I guess God was showing me what I was holding in." He swallowed and swiped at his eyes again. "You got a bit too close for comfort and I pushed ya away."

"I forgive ya, of course I do!" Ailsa said, "I was shocked myself to see what God showed me. I think I saw you, like He sees ya, on the inside, I mean, all broken and wounded and full of pain. But of course, I didnae know He was goin' to change ya just like tha'!" she laughed. "He did the same for me and my da' about two years ago. I'm still learnin' for sure, but I wouldnae go back."

"And do I ever have a story for you about how God came into my life!" Socorro piped in, laughing. "Looks like we have lots to talk about."

The group then dispersed after a prayer of Thanksgiving. Nothing more needed to be said.

God had visited them in the most unexpected way, through the salvation of a stranger.

~

Angels rejoiced in the heavens! The joy and thanksgiving the group felt on earth expanded to the vast spiritual realm. Another victory for the light! "Hallelujah," they cried. "Hallelujah."

CHAPTER 9

GETTING ACQUAINTED

Socorro was concentrating on the job at hand as he snapped pictures near the lighthouse. The only sounds heard were the small hum of his drone and the lapping waves. It was a clear, cool morning with absolutely no mist, which was rare for this time of year on the island. He took advantage of the perfect light and honed in on the nest. Three tiny eggs in that one! He snapped a half dozen shots of the nest, then he widened the angle and got a few shots of the light house from a bird's eye view. Kristal was going to love these!

He directed the drone on, searching for birds. He loved catching them in flight, their wings spread wide in the early morning sun. His spirit soared with theirs, as his device flew alongside them. The video captured these moments perfectly, but he waited until just the right moment to capture their still image with the camera. The birds had become used to the hum of the drone. After all, he had been doing this for over a year now.

When Socorro decided to become a drone pilot, he found there were many steps to it. He had to take classes, which his dad helped him sign up for. Then he had to travel by ferry to the mainland each week to attend these classes. A six-hour trip one way!

But he studied hard and was finally able to obtain the license required to fly the drone. He paid for it all himself. It made him feel accomplished and something his dad required. Since he had worked many hours for it, he was invested in the project and he felt more responsible. He took good care of the equipment. It was expensive, after all, and he didn't want to have to replace it.

The photos he took were used in a nonprofit that he and his sister had started. He took the raw photos, then she edited and uploaded them for print. Together they had opened a small shop in the castle where they sold tee shirts, postcards and posters with the birds or other wildlife featured on them. Hamish, in his spare time, opened an online shop and helped them sell the products that way. All of the money earned went back into the conservation of the wildlife on *Mystic Island*.

There were plenty of photo opportunities here. The wildlife was almost endless! Sea creatures, ponies, cows, foxes and birds were abundant on the island. But the puffins were his favorite subjects to photograph, with the snowy owl and the highland cows next in popularity.

He had initially thought about inviting Rory Tibbetts to come along with him this morning, but as he left, he noticed that Ailsa and Rory were still in their rooms.

That boy's past was still a mystery to him. After the devotion last night, Rory was given an extra set of Socorro's pj's and sent to bed. Dad said there would be time to figure everything out later, when they were all rested.

Socorro lost track of time and space as he followed the wildlife. All he knew was he was capturing fantastic video on this clear morning! He followed the flight of the birds with the drone until he found himself way up on the beach.

He glanced down at his watch. Yikes! It was almost time for breakfast. He'd better hurry!

He shut the drone down and headed home. It was a school day, which meant a tight schedule. But he dreaded going inside. Nothing in his studies compared to being outside exploring!

He entered the castle through the back door, stomping into the kitchen, as was his nature. His parents said he was always in a hurry. But there was so much of life to live and things to do! It wasn't his fault he had so much energy!

Ailsa sat at the kitchen table, yawning and rubbing the sleep from her eyes. Her hair was smoothed back into a ponytail, her glasses folded up and laid beside her plate. There was a time when she would have been up and outside with him, but of late, she seemed to be less energetic.

He went to the big utility sink and washed his hands; his drone tucked under one arm. Tossing his head to get his long hair out of his eyes, he scrubbed up.

He plopped down in the chair next to Ailsa. She frowned at him. "Why do ya still have the drone? Better move it so nothing spills on all that equipment!"

He sighed, peeved at Ailsa. He pushed his chair back and put the drone and the controller on a table in the pantry. Even though Ailsa was right, she didn't need to be so grumpy and bossy. He always thought of his big sister as the bossy one. But now, when she was gone all week, he was still bossed around! And by someone younger than he. *Life was not fair!*

The family joined in the morning prayer. Still no Tibbetts. *Was he sleeping through breakfast too?* "Mom, where's Rory? Isn't he going to eat this morning?" Socorro asked.

"Well, I gave him the breakfast times last night and he said he'd be here, so I'm not sure."

"Hmm, missing in action again," Socorro said.

But as they started passing around the food, he appeared. "Pardon me for being late. I wasnae sure of the time since I donnae own a watch, so I used me nose to tell me when it was time to eat! Somethin' smells brill!"

Was this the Rory Tibbetts they saw last night? He looked entirely different this morning. His honey-colored, shoulder length hair was washed and combed, parted neatly down the middle. He had on fresh clothes, too, thanks to Mom — She had raided Socorro's and Dad's closet to come up with a set. He held his head high and made eye contact. He smiled shyly, his deep blue eyes sparkling.

Socorro invited him to sit beside him. They all scooted around and made room. He was dying to ask the boy questions!

As they ate, Socorro started his interrogation. "Now, fill me in on where you came from!" he blurted.

Ailsa, sitting on the other side of Socorro, jabbed him with her elbow. "Donnae ya think that can wait until after breakfast?"

He rolled his eyes at Miss bossy again. "Yeah, sorry. I'm just excited to get to know him!"

"It's okay," Rory said. "I owe yous an explanation. But where do I start? I guess first off, I need to tell ya that I only took the food and such to survive. I'm nae a thief. In fac' I plan to work and pay ya back. Yous have been very kind. I'm a hard worker. Before landing here, I worked as a deckhand on a tramp steamer. But that went south, and no fault of me own either!"

Dad spoke up. "I'm sure you are a hard worker. But what's important now is how you got here. How old are you, son? You can't be much older than Socorro, here. If something happened to him, we'd be desperate to know where he was. Is someone looking for you? Your parent's, or other family?"

"No, I'm an orphan. Me mum died when I was but a wee lad. Me dad, passed on last year. Once he died, I hit the streets and lived hand to mouth. There's a whole lot of us in the same fix. But I got plenty tired of livin' on the streets. Gangs and robbers are always after ya and make it dangerous. If I hadnae been good at hidin', I wouldnae be here, noo." He stopped to chew his food, which he'd scooped up hungrily. After he swallowed, he continued. "I wanted to work and stay away from the street gangs. I heard aboot this job on the tramp steamer; tha' they was hirin' deckhands. But I think I got in with a bad bunch of blokes! They pushed me and knocked me around. Again, I hid ou'. One day after I'd been on board a few months, I heard the Cap'n say he was runnin' dope and contraband. Noo tha's too much, even for a street lad!"

Tibbetts took a big swallow of his milk, swiped his mouth with the back of his hand and wiped it on his jeans.

"I decided I had to get off the ship. One night, when I was pullin' in rope, I saw a strange light reflecting on the water. I looked up and there was a lighthouse! It was my chance. I decided to swim to the shore. Luckily, the crew were passed out from the drink. The ship got closer and closer to the shore. It was dark and the opportunity was perfect, so I jumped!"

"How long ago? I mean, have you been hiding long?" Mom asked.

"I'm nae sure, maybe jist a few days ago. I woke up on the beach and saw them deliverin' food to the lighthouse." He indicated Socorro and Ailsa with the nod of his head.

"I was starvin', so I pinched it." His eyes dropped to his plate. "I'm sorry, and as I said before, I'll work to pay for it. Please forgive me."

"Pinched it?" Socorro asked, not familiar with that term.

"Aye, pinchin' is takin' it without permission. Yous say stealin'" Ailsa explained.

Gee, who had joined them for breakfast this morning, piped up. "Oh! So tha's wha' happened ta' my breakfast! Finally, the mystery is solved. We were ready ta' blame the dog!" he chuckled. "But if ya had shown yourself and told us the truth at the start, we could've saved ya a lot of grief. We would've gladly fed ya."

"I was too scared yous would turn me in to the authorities. I donnae have an ID or passport."

"Oh, yeah. How old did ya say ya were, lad?" Gee asked.

"I'm fifteen. Almost legal." Rory replied, lifting his chin.

"I'm fourteen," Socorro told him. "Even though I wish I was out on my own, I know I'm not ready yet. I'm thankful for my family and friends. I'm sorry your parents died and now your all alone." He paused and all the family around the table agreed. Socorro continued, "And although my story is different, I know what it means to be in a tough spot. My sister and I were lost on a mountain a few years back and we had to survive on our own for several weeks. If it wasn't for God, who helped us find our family, we would probably still be there! But He had other plans for us. We know that now. It was just about a year later, when we mysteriously inherited this castle! You never know what's going to happen."

Rory nodded. He had so many unexpected things happen to him. He would've never dreamed he'd be here right now. He pushed his empty plate back. He'd eaten everything but the fork.

"Rory, will you join me in my office? I have just a few more questions for you." Dad asked, getting up. He smiled at the lad to help him feel at ease.

The family pushed back from the table. Ailsa and Socorro had chores and lessons to do, and the rest had a business to run. Even though hearing about Rory's life was more interesting, getting better acquainted with him would have to come later. Duty calls, as they say.

CHAPTER 10

THE CHOSEN ONE

Tibbetts wiggled in the chair in Kris' office. *I bet they'll throw me ou' of here! The coppers will be here soon, and I'll pay for pinchin' their stuff,* he worried. He pushed his hair behind his ears and bit his lip. His gut tightened. After feeling so light and free after the encounter he had had last night, fear and doubt was creeping in.

Kris smiled to put the boy at ease. "Listen, you're not in trouble with me. But I have to be responsible and check out your story. And to do that I'll need some information from you. If you write down your name, your parents' names and your birth date, I can find out more about you. I'll also need all your past addresses. Just a quick check on the internet and then we'll go from there." Kris handed him a tablet and a pen. "Another thing to think about, what about school? Have you finished your studies?"

"No, sir. I was on track until me da' passed. After tha' I didnae even try to go to school. But I finished key stage 3, meanin' I have one stage left to finish."

"Hmm, let me figure this out. I want you to know I'll do my best to help you. I'm sorry you've had such a hard go of it. No kid deserves to grow up on the streets. And about last evening, I want you to know I'll help mentor you in any way I can as you learn to be a Christ follower. But please, you'll have to let us do that. That means you need to trust us. No more hiding and running."

"Yes. I've had enough of that meself." He took the pad of paper and the pen Kris offered. He wrote down everything he could remember, then handed it back to Kris.

"Now go find Socorro and have him show you around the place. I think you'll find he and Ailsa will be a great help to you and hopefully you'll all be good pals. I'll get started on this bit of research, then we'll talk again soon. In the meantime, make yourself at home."

Tibbetts scooted out of the chair. "Ta, I will. I'm glad for the help. It'd be brill if I can work here and really start over." He opened the office door. As he left, he stuck his head back in and said, "And thanks for nae throwin' me ou'." He shut the door, then and scurried off.

Tibbetts returned to the kitchen where Adara and Mary were working on menus. "I was wonderin' if yous know where the lad and lass have got off to?" he asked.

"I'll take you to them, Rory. Is it alright if I call you Rory?" Adara asked, placing her hand on his shoulder and leading him toward the door.

"Yes, I was called Rory by me family. Tibbetts was me street name. But since I'm at a new place, I'll go by my given name." *Why not? Maybe here I can shed some of my past.* He was certainly hopeful he could, anyway.

He followed Adara up the staircase and to the library where the kids had just settled down to watch a required video. They were lounging in the overstuffed chairs, Ailsa's cat curled up in her lap. When they arrived, the cat jumped up, startled.

"Ailsa, Socorro, I have a new assignment for you," Mom said as she came through the arched opening of the massive library.

Socorro groaned. *What now?* It was hard to keep a good attitude when they kept piling on the book work!

Adara gave him a crooked grin, "It's a good assignment. I think both of you will like what I'm about to say. How about I give you a day off from studying so you two can show Rory around and help him feel at home? This place is big and can be overwhelming. I think he needs a tour."

Socorro jumped up and pumped his fist into the air. "Of course we'll show him around. Can we visit the cows and puffins, too?"

"If you think you can do all that before lunch, go for it. Or maybe show him around outside this morning and after lunch, you can tour the castle." she suggested.

"For sure! We have some very special pals for ya to meet," Ailsa said as she powered off her tablet. "And there are puppies! We have to take ya to see the pups!"

Adara laughed. "I thought you'd like the new plans. Lunch is at half-past noon as usual, so try not to be late. With so many guests here right now, we really need to be strict on the schedule. I have one birdwatcher that is O.C.D. with the times. He marks the schedule down, then complains if were even a minute late." She shook her head. Socorro knew how hard it was to keep the guests happy. He'd had his share of unpleasant encounters with them.

"So, where should we start? Do you want to check out the garden area?"

"Naw, I've seen the garden. Some of those days I was hidin' out, well, I was in your garden."

"Hey, you didn't happen to borrow a couple of towels, did ya?" Socorro asked.

"Guilty! Guess I'd better add that to the tab of things I will pay for." Rory said, sheepishly.

"It's okay. But now I know I'm not going crazy! When Ailsa said she didn't take them, I thought maybe I forgot to bring them or something! Glad the mystery is solved." He held up his palm for a 'high five' and Rory obliged.

"Great! Let's get the quad bikes and head to the cliffs, then. We have some cool places to show ya." Ailsa said. She was excited and looking forward to a day without studies.

As she ran ahead to the garage, Rory asked Socorro a question. "I've never had a sister or anything, but she's what, around twelve? Isn't she a pain to hang around? Do you feel like a babysitter?"

Socorro's eyes widened. Ailsa could be a pain, but they actually enjoyed each other's company most of the time. "Well, I guess we are used to each other. She's really a lot of fun, once ya get to know her. You'll see, she's pretty cool, even though she is just twelve."

"Well, we'll see. I've been impressed by the way she sings. I'd say she is better than anyone I've heard lately. Does she sing every night at the gathering?" Rory asked. But they had just arrived at the garage, so there was no further opportunity to discuss Ailsa.

Ailsa and Socorro each got on a four-wheeler. "Hope you know how to handle one of these," Socorro said as he tossed the key to Rory. His dad had recently added a few more of the vehicles to his collection so there was one for each of them.

"Uh, no, but I'll figure it ou'." He shouted to their backs as the two peeled off toward the cliffs. He got on, donned the helmet and turned the key. He squeezed the handles to engage the throttle and lurched forward. *Jerk, jerk, jerk.* The engine died. He tried again, shifting it into gear. He sped off, although not very smoothly. He followed in their tracks. He was determined not be left in the dust!

When they all arrived at the cliffs, Rory was relieved he'd made it there safely and with his dignity still intact. He was gaining respect for both of these kids. He was street smart, but out here in the open terrain, there would be a learning curve. They definitely knew how to handle the quad bikes!

"Okay, let me tell ya something about these birds," Socorro started. But Ailsa interrupted him.

"Aye ya should, but that is rather blunt, donnae think? Wha' Socorro meant to say is, let us introduce ya to the puffins."

"For sure! I *meant* to tell you these are not ordinary puffins, ya know?" Socorro said, walking toward the cliffs.

Rory looked confused. *Wha' are they talkin' aboot?*

"Here, let me show ya!" Ailsa ran ahead to the precipice. They could hear the deep calls of the massive bird flock over the waves. She put her fingers in her mouth and produced a loud, shrill whistle. As a group, the birds silenced.

Suddenly, one of the black and white birds landed at her feet. The orange of its beak was as vivid as the black of its feathers was dark. She knelt down and gave it a pat, and a gentle hug. "Hello Deemer. I brought a new friend to meet ya. He is one of us, so you can feel safe around him. His name is Rory. Are you okay with that?"

The bird studied Rory for a moment. It flew up and looked him straight in the eyes and he could smell the fishiness of it. He felt tempted to swat it away, like a pesky fly! But then the bird opened its bright orange beak and spoke to him.

"I think I already know ya! Youse the one who swam out of the ocean and onto the beach, covered in seaweed. Wha' a mess you was! Thankfully some of my pals in the sea helped ya along, or ya wouldnae have made it! Did ya know tha'?" the bird asked, speaking loudly above the noise of the sea. Rory just starred, finding himself in complete shock.

"Well, they did. As you got close to shore, the dolphins stirred the wake to carry you in faster so ya wouldnae drown. They understand how important it is to get air, because dolphins have to breathe just like you.

Our creator has a purpose for ya, to be sure." she said, as she backed off a bit.

Rory knew his mouth was hanging open. *These are very different birds! And to find out that the dolphins helped me, well, I'm jist grateful.* Maybe he *did* matter to someone or at least something. And of course, there was the spiritual experience last night that reaffirmed that.

"I'm nae sure wha' to say! But you're right, I was exhausted and drownin'." Overcome with emotion, he sat down on the ground, cross-legged and put his face in his hands.

Ailsa came over and put her hand on his shoulder. "You, okay?" she said softly.

Rory took in a couple of deep breaths. So much had happened in the past couple of days and his future was still so unsure, he wasn't okay! But as we all do in such situations he replied, "Yeah, I'm okay. Jist give me a minute."

Deemer, standing near him, continued to speak. "Here on this terra firma, there are problems and sorrows. But in heaven, everything is fixed! There's no sorrow, pain or death there! Nae even a tear will fall." —She paused to see if he was taking all this in. Then she continued to speak as she walked around— "The earth is a mess! Sin sickness is putrid and is dripping from all the human creatures, covering them in filth, until the Creator cleans them up!" She fluttered about a bit and then landed in front of him again. She took a deep breath, then continued. "Some of your kind, humans I mean, choose to wallow in it and try to find their own way." She shook her head. "But you found the cleansin' didnae ya?" Rory just stared at her, not knowing how to answer.

"I sense it. But there's more to come. You're in for more revelations, soon. All the pain and sorrow you have encountered in your life has emptied you. Noo it's time to be filled back up again. The Creator has planned that you be here, at this very time and this very place! Oh, what a mission He has for you!" the bird then took wing, "Bye, chosen one!"

She flew away rapidly; her bright orange feet tucked beneath her belly. They watched as she soared in the gentle wind, riding the breeze down to the sea where she dove in, her body traveling fluidly in the waves.

Then Socorro and Ailsa sat on the ground with him, forming a circle.

Rory cautiously looked up. "This is the strangest place I've ever been, but in a gud way. That bird speaks truth, 'cause I do feel like I'm being filled back up. Last night, I felt somethin' I've never felt before. You know wha' I mean, right?" His heart rate had increased, and his cheeks burned. He was not used to being so open and vulnerable.

Both kids nodded, "For sure we do! But just wait! It gets better with time." Socorro said.

"Sometimes when I worship," Ailsa said quietly, "I feel like I cross from this realm to the next one, where God lives. It took a long time to happen, but it happened when I learned to draw close to Him."

"Yeah. I agree." Socorro said, standing. "But I really want you to meet some other pals of ours. Are ya up for it?" he asked.

Was he? He felt pretty overwhelmed right now. But he nodded yes. How could he pass up another eye-opening adventure?

CHAPTER 11

THE NEWS

Meanwhile on the island near the shipping docks, a creature stirred. *Jeepers*, the wee colorful pine marten, hunkered down in the heather.

Boom boom boom!

It's so much noisier than before! Them sea vessels docking here has spoiled the peace! This island used to be so quiet...Screeeech! He jumped. He rose to his hind legs and put his wee paws over his ears. When the noise level lessened, he dropped to his four paws and skedaddled!

He ran, not fast, but steadily. Soon he arrived in the field between the coos and the Clydesdales, the monsters of the shire dell. He had news and tha's what the big ones wanted. He didnae get paid for his information, but he was revered for it. He felt like a prince, no, a king among the creatures! Wee but mighty! And besides, there were lots of field mice aboot. Yum!

"Pssst, pssst." Jeepers said as he joined the coos.

"Look, Mum, it's the wee cat!" Belgium, the newest wee coo, announced.

Ugh! Jeepers hated it when he called him a cat! "I'm a marten, ya dum-dum..." he whispered to himself. He dare nae say it louder, those coo mums could get downright vicious!

"Hi ya, Jeepers. We didnae see ya. You tend to creep up on us soooo unexpectedly." Lulabelle said as she chewed her cud. "Goooot news? We'd love to hear it, gud or bad!"

"Aye, ya bet I got news! But it's scary, creepy news. Yous better send the wee one away." Jeepers turned and glanced around him, his bright yellow belly gleaming in the sun. He was hoping he hadn't been followed. No amount of caution was too much. Not when it came to the "eyes".

"Off with ya, then," Annika said to Belgium.

"Moooo, but Ah'll miss all the fun!" he complained as he sauntered off. They waited until he was out of hearing range to continue.

"Noo, give us the tale, and make sure it's true!" Lulabelle insisted.

Jeepers walked back and forth nervously. He usually spoke with the Clydesdales first, but with the wee calf aboot, this lot were the ones in the most danger.

"I saw this with my own eyes, so it's truth with a capitol 'T'!" Jeepers emphasized. "Like I'd tell ya tall tales, really?" he said, offended.

"Well, go on then," Annika prompted.

"I was down by the bay, huntin'." he said, sounding mysterious. "It was dark, no moon a' tall. The water was restless and noisy, and it kept me on alert! It was then I saw these enormous red lights out over the bay, way off, in the distance. They were in pairs, like eyes staring at me! There must have been dozens! I donnae if it was sea creatures, or ghost creatures, or wha'!" he paused and looked at his audience. The coos were tuned in, tails a waggin'.

"Donnae keep us in suspense! Wha' was it? Creatures, ghosts, oooor maybe even fairies!" Lulabelle said, speaking slowly and drawn out, which was her norm.

"I jist told ya! I donnae know wha' it were. But it werenae gud! Yous know I care aboot the wee coo, and I wanted ya to be the first to know aboot this. Keep an eye out, for sure!"

"...and the Clydesdales say they saw wolves aboot!" Jeepers yelled, as he turned and ran across the glen.

His job was done for now, and it was up to those silly coos to heed his warning or not! As for him and his kind, caution was the word!

Chapter 12

Pals

The kids ran back to the four-wheelers and in a flash, they headed toward the castle. They sped as fast as they dared and soon arrived at the drive just outside the garage. Ailsa and Rory waited as Socorro ran into the castle for something. Soon he reappeared with a paper bag.

"I know better than to show up without treats." he said. Ailsa nodded. They pulled out and turned right onto a rough dirt road that led away from the castle. Rory was learning the importance of the ATVs. They were needed in this terrain for sure.

The three traveled in tandem, and Rory felt proud of himself for catching on so quickly. He took a deep breath, gulping in the fresh air. Although chilly, it smelled fresh and clean, unlike the sooty air of the city. They continued down the dirt road, rushing past fenced fields, feasting their eyes on miles of green pastures speckled with livestock. The white woolly sheep and the cinnamon-colored cows were the only creatures around, except for an occasional bird flying by.

Socorro slowed and then stopped in what Rory considered the middle of nowhere. He parked the vehicle on the side of the road and the others followed suit.

"Be careful and donnae touch the fence. It is electrified." Ailsa called out to Rory, as she hopped over a narrow drainage ditch and walked toward an empty field.

"Why did we stop here? There's nothing around, that I can see."

Ailsa laughed. "Jist wait!"

Socorro stood near the fence and shook the bag. Something rattled inside and the bag made a crackling noise. Rory shielded his eyes with his hand and gazed across the tall, grassy, field. He saw movement in the grass, then in the distance a wee herd of highland coos became visible and moseyed toward them. The leader began to trot when it saw them. Soon, they were all trotting across the field making a beeline straight for them.

"Now you're in for another cool surprise! These coos are so fun to be around." Socorro chuckled.

He reached into the bag and pulled out an apple. He handed it to Ailsa and then got two more out for himself and Rory.

"Mooove it, lassies! They've got treats!" the lead coo called out, her breath visible in the cool air.

Again, Rory's jaw dropped! *Talking cows?* He hung back from the fence a bit, not knowing what to expect. Life in Liverpool was tough, but at least he knew what was happening. Here, there was a surprise a minute!

Ailsa waved to the coos. "Come over and let's visit!"

"Beeee right there! Ah seeee ya got some treats for us! And have weeee got some news for yooooous!"

The kids held out the apples as the coos approached the fence, carefully avoiding the wires.

"We brought a pal, but he's friendly, so donnae get nervous," Ailsa warned them. "This is Rory, and Rory, this is Lulabelle, Annika and the wee white one with the black nose and ears, is Annika's calf, Belgium. Guess where his dad came from?" They all chuckled.

"Ah'm pleased to meeet ya." Lulabelle cooed. She turned toward the others, "But Ah hope he knows that we donnae jist speak to anyone and he must promise to neva tell anyone that we can speak with humans!" She looked sternly at Ailsa and Socorro.

"Yeah, believe me, I'm nae plannin' on tellin' anyone I've been chattin' with coos!" He couldn't help but grin at the irony. They were afraid of being found out, but he was more afraid of seeming daft!

After the coos ate all the fruit Socorro brought, he asked them what news they had.

Annika spoke up. "Git along over the way, Belgium, this is not news for wee ears!" Belgium slowly wandered off, glancing behind him as he went. When he was gone, she continued. "Well, Ah've been speaking with the Clydesdale's. They claim that there is danger aboot! Wolves!" she shouted, a bit of her cud falling from her mouth.

"Where? Where are the Clydesdales, I mean?" Ailsa inquired.

Lulabelle answered. "Oooover in the field next to this one, way back over there. We speak throoough the fence. But we didnae speak directly with them, but from a messenger, which shall remain unnamed." She blinked and nodded.

"Well, I donnae believe them! There arenae any wolves in Scotland and especially on this island!" Ailsa shouted. "I believe they're tellin' tall tales!"

"Wait, what if something weird happened and some poachers, or someone else, brought in wolves? I dealt with wolves on *Mystic Mountain*, and I sure don't want to see them again!" Socorro shivered.

"Well, Ah donnae if they're real wolves, oooor they're talkin' aboot evil beings. But evil is aboot! Yous can count on that! Scary red eyeees!" Annika nodded her big furry head, her long hair shaking about.

Rory gasped! *The crew of the tramp steamer! What if they are on the island lookin' for me?* He spoke directly to Annika. "You need to find out! Please! Find out if it's evil humans or animals. There were pirates and drug dealers on that steamer I was on! What if they're here lookin' for me?" Rory looked over his shoulder and shivered. If they found him, he was a goner.

"Nooo donnae get worked up, laddie. Annika likes to exaggerate a bit. Ah'll get to the bottom of it if ya bring us more of thooose treats!" Lulabelle said.

"Mooooove quickly with the treats," Belgium spoke out, in his sweet baby voice. Apparently, he had snuck back unnoticed. Ailsa carefully reached through the wires and petted his soft head. She loved the babies. And he was so beautiful! His coat color reminded her of Belgium cream!

"Yeah, we'll be back as soon as we can. With schoolwork and chores, we don't have much free time. But this new information is scary! Ailsa has wee sheep! And what about all the sheep still out in the fields? It's not cold enough to put them in the barns yet. They would all be in danger if wolves are about!" Socorro rambled.

Ailsa shook her head. "I'm nae worried. As far as I know, wolves are extinct here and how could anyone bring them in?"

"Well, I don't want to be negative, but poachers sneak up in boats all the time. They could bring them in and turn them loose! We'll just have to be more alert! If they're here, I'll find them with my drone."

"But Ah say donnae worry yet! Roooomers are common here with the coos and the Clydesdales, too. I think the message came from the Clydesdales, but maybe it came from the messenger. If it were from him, well you can take that with a lick of salt! Tha' wee marten could go either way, truth to tales, who knows! We're all so bored tha' when we see other beasties, the taaaales fly!" Lulabelle chuckled.

"Well, Ah nevah!" Annika pretended to be insulted. But it looked like she gave Belgium a firm wink!

"Let's get back. I'm cold and it's almost lunch time. Remember what your mum said aboot being late! Bye coos!" Ailsa called.

The kids hopped on the four-wheelers and sped off. Rory watched the coos in his rear-view mirror until they were out of sight. *Wow, jist wow!* He was over the moon! Talking birds and beasties! The visit was amazing but the message they shared was terrifying! He hoped he'd never see those pirates again! He'd rather face a ferocious wolf! He shivered, involuntarily. Hopefully it was just a rumor or tall tale. But deep down, he knew. He was being WATCHED!

CHAPTER 13

THE DOOR

Back at the castle, the group gathered in the kitchen for lunch. Everyone was chattering cheerfully. The aroma rising from the steaming bowls made Rory's mouth water. He could barely wait for the blessing to be finished before he dug in. He helped himself to a huge bowl of steaming pea soup. He was tempted to gobble it down, but he paced himself, since his body was not used to so much food. He'd felt a wee bit sick after he wolfed down his breakfast, earlier. The abundance of food here was almost overwhelming.

When the bowls were collected and sugary biscuits were passed around, Kris clamped his hand on Rory's shoulder. "I'd like to see you in my office for just a few minutes. Finish your lunch, then stop in." He sounded calm enough and Tibbetts tried not to read too much into it. But his stomach knotted just the same.

He wrapped a couple of freshly baked sweets in a napkin and took them with him. He'd eat them later. For now, he'd lost his appetite.

"Ready to check the place out?" Socorro asked, crunching on a cookie.

"I need to see your dad first. He said it wouldn't take long. Can I meet you guys upstairs in the library?"

"Sure," Ailsa said. "But why donnae we stop in to see the puppies, first? You can meet us in Socorro's Grammy's and Pop's room. It's room 303."

Tibbetts knocked on the office door. He felt his knees trembling. *Better just man up and get this over with,* he told himself. *He swallowed.*

"Come in," Kris called. He was busy at the computer, but turned to face Tibbetts as he came in. "Have a seat and leave the door open. I have good news."

Tibbetts released a long breath he hadn't realized he was holding. "Wha' news do ya have, then?" he asked as he lowered himself into the chair.

"I did a background and history check, and I found your mom and dad's obituaries. Your story checks out. But I didn't find any other family listed. I'm sorry, Rory." Kris's eyes showed his sincerity. "But judging from last night's experience, I think things are definitely looking up for you. And when you're ready, let me know. I'd like to talk to you more about it. Our family will help in any way we can."

"You're not call'n the coppers?" Rory asked.

"No, I searched both names you gave us, and Rory Tibbetts was the only name that showed up. It even showed a picture of you, taken after you played in a football tournament and made the winning score."

"Yes, tha's before Da' passed. Back when I was just a regular lad. But after he was gone, I was nae sure wha' to do so I took to the streets before the courts could assign me to somewhere I didnae want to go. I was too old to stay in a care home, and who wants to take in a teenage lad? It were easy to hide in the city." Rory explained.

"I'll get our lawyer to advise us, but you can stay here for now, if you want. I think at your age you can choose where you want to live, and hopefully you'll want to stay here with us. Again, I'll check into everything."

Tibbetts sighed. "Wow, that sounds great! But like I said this mornin', I can work. I want to repay ya for your kindness to me. And I want to learn more about God and such." Rory stared off, thinking on what the puffin said. *He was chosen.* He shook his head to clear it.

Kris smiled. The boy already seemed to be on the right track. "I'll make sure you have you're own copy of the Bible to read. Ailsa and Socorro start the day reading the Bible and praying and they will be glad to help you as you start this journey. As for working, let's put that off a bit. School work is more important right now. We'll get the tutor to set up a study plan for you so you can finish. If you study hard, that will be all the pay I need right now."

"Thank you, sir. I'm grateful for yous kindness." Not knowing what else to say, he smiled and left. He took the stairs up to room 303. He knocked quietly on the door.

"Come on in," Pop invited. The kids were lying on the floor, puppies climbing all over them. There was an abundance of giggling and wee yaps.

Rory smiled at the mountain of fur. He bent down and a wee brindle pup lumbered up to him. He sat down and scooped it up. He smoothed its soft fur with his fingers and accepted the pup's kisses in return.

When the puppies began to tire, Pop called Foster over to her bed. The puppies snuggled up to their mum, enjoying their afternoon feast.

"Since you've met most of our animal pals, now we'll show ya around the castle!"

"Come on!" Ailsa called, already charging out of the door.

The kids chatted excitedly as they wandered around the castle, showing Rory the many nooks and crannies. They even showed him the secret passageway they'd found while running from a mysterious guest. They had accidentally fallen through the wall into the hidden passage!

"Wow! So, there's more than one." Rory said. "I found one, too, in the hall. It leads into the pantry in the kitchen. I found it while hidin' out. I'll show yous when we go back down."

"Great! I knew there had to be more of them! Maybe we will find even more today!" Ailsa said.

“I wouldnae doubt it! Makes ya wonder wha’ went on here in the past! Can ya imagine living in a castle on a hill on an island?” Rory said. They laughed.

Soon, after many steep steps, they found themselves on the very top floor. They examined every nook and crack looking for secret doors that led to other rooms. That’s when they happened upon a thick wooden door none of them had seen before. It was hidden in a dark corner shadowed by the turret and tucked out of sight. Dust and cobwebs hung like sheets over the surface. It didn’t have a handle, just a hole where a knob or latch used to be. Ailsa peeked through the hole, but it was too dark to see inside. She jumped back, startled, after feeling a cold breeze.

“Wha’s wrong?” Rory asked.

“Cold air is pouring through the hole! This door must lead to the outside! I donnae remember seeing any door up here from the outside, but then, you cannae really see this far up from the garden, can ya? Castles are so mysterious with all their crooks and turns.”

“Probably can’t see it from outside because of all the gables and such. Plus, we weren’t actually looking for a door. Let’s see if we can get it open!” Socorro suggested. He paused. He suddenly remembered that he almost fell down an empty elevator shaft when they first came to the castle. He had promised his dad then that he would be careful when inspecting unknown places. “Ailsa, quick, run down to your room and get a flashlight. Let’s shine it in before we open the door. I don’t feel like falling off the highest point of the castle this afternoon!”

Rory laughed. “Well, no, nae a good plan.”

Ailsa sighed. Socorro was being pretty bossy.

“Please, Ailsa?” he said, realizing his error.

Ailsa nodded, then turned down the hall to the back stairwell.

While she was gone, Rory asked Socorro a random question, "How old are those pups? Do ya have homes for all of them or are you keeping the whole liter?"

"We still have a couple of weeks until they are weaned. That reminds me that we need to find homes for them. Mom already said we can't keep them all. Why?"

"I know this sounds crazy, but do you think I could have one? I've neva' had a pet. When we were in there pettin' them, the idea popped into my head!" he laughed. "If I get to stay, that is. Your dad says he is gonna help me. I hope it works out." Rory grew quiet, pondering what it would be like to belong somewhere and have a wee dog that belonged to him!

"That would be cool. I hope you can stay, because I've never had a brother."

Clump, clump, clump! Ailsa had returned, out of breath. "Here, move over, Socorro, let me shine the torch in the hole!"

"I want to look first! Give it to me, Ailsa." Socorro said. Pushing her away.

"Oh no ya donnae! I went for it." And before he could take it, she pushed back and flipped it on. She directed the beam inside the hole. They all waited in anticipation until she suddenly dropped the flashlight and screamed! They all jumped back.

"What did ya see?" the boys asked at once. But she was gone, running like a gazelle down the hall. They looked at each other and Rory picked up the flashlight. It was busted. "Oh man! No use trying to see in there noo."

The lads stood there for a moment deciding what to do next when they heard an eerie sound. A sound of heavy breathing escaped through the hole in the door! The boys looked at each other with wide terrified eyes and flew out after Alisa!

So much for being strong and brave! Socorro thought as they arrived downstairs out of breath. He should have marched himself back up there and checked it out, but instead he questioned Ailsa.

"Outside," she pointed to the door. "Let's go out and I'll tell ya!" she whispered.

She started running as soon as her feet hit the portico. She was almost out of sight when the boys realized how far ahead, she was. They ran after her, their long legs flying.

Ailsa disappeared around the corner of the castle. She passed by her wee sheep who started baaing loudly when they saw her. The sudden movement and the noisy sheep startled her cat, who had been sunning herself on the fence. She screeched, and with all claws out, she flew right onto Rory's face. He yelped! Ailsa skidded to a stop and turned to look back at the ruckus. Socorro was trying to help Rory rid himself of the cat, but she had dug her claws into his skin. The frightened animal ended up scratching both boys on their arms and cheeks, until they finally pulled her away. She jumped down and disappeared behind the house. The boys stopped to examine their wounds.

"Oh no," Ailsa gasped. "Yous are bleedin'!" she yelled over all the animal noises.

Adara stuck her head out the back door. "What's going on out here? Come on in, it's time to eat."

As the kids came in to wash up, the boys cleaned their scratches, which proved to be minor, and gathered around the table. Strange doors, turrets and mysterious sounds would have to wait.

After the blessing, Socorro brought up the question that was foremost on his mind.

"What did you see up there and why did you run like you did?" he asked Ailsa. Since everyone was chatting and not listening to them, she quietly told them.

"Well, when I looked through the hole, the light caught two red eyes! They looked like devil eyes! And they looked right at me!" she shivered. "I think it was a wolf!

"But how could a wolf get up that high?" Rory asked. "Wait! That reminds me of something! Red eyes, you said? I saw the same red eyes when I jumped off the tramp steamer! But instead of one set, there were dozens! But they were looking at me from the ship!"

"And wasn't it red eyes that the coos were talkin' about?" Socorro said.

Alisa nodded her head. "But it makes no sense! As I said before, there are no wolves here. Tha's where I was going when I ran! I wanted to see if I could spot the door from outside. But my view was blocked by the balcony and turrets."

"There's got to be a logical explanation. For the eyes and noises! But then the wee sheep started baaing and you know the rest!" Rory said.

Picturing the crazy chain of events with the cat, activated Rory's funny bone. He started to laugh! He laughed and laughed and laughed! He knew he was being rude, acting so silly at the table, but he couldn't stop! His humor spigot had turned on and there was no off button.

His laugh was contagious and soon Ailsa and Socorro joined in. Socorro's parents just shook their heads.

Pop gave them a stern look.

Kris finally spoke up. "Since you guys obviously have no control over whatever has amused you, I think you are excused from the table. Come back for dessert once you feel better."

This statement brought on more laughter. They pushed back from the table and made it out the back door, still bent over with glee.

The fresh air seemed to help, and they calmed down. The laughter had been a relief after the weird day!

"The wee sheep are hungry for their supper, so I'll go feed them," Ailsa announced. "Want to help me?"

But the boys were preoccupied with their own conversation and sat down on the concrete step. "Well, I think you got a pretty good tour of the castle today! Maybe we saw more than any of us wanted!" Socorro said.

"Yes. I'm not sure wha' scared Ailsa, but I'm sure it wasn't a wolf! How would it get up there? I'm sure there is a reasonable explanation." Rory mused. *But the heavy breathing?* He wasn't sure if there was a reasonable explanation for that!

The boys sat quietly, pondering the mystery as they watched Ailsa. She filled the feed trough for the lambs as well as their drinking pan with water. The sun was setting and the temperature was starting to drop, making them anxious to go inside.

"We'll need to talk more later. Why don't you come to my room after devotionals, and we'll talk. If you're okay with that." Socorro said.

Rory shrugged. "Sure, I've nothing else planned and we can get better acquainted."

The kids cleaned up and changed, ready for devotionals. Rory felt his spirit lift when they mentioned it was time to go down. He was hungry to learn more!

"Hey, kiddos," Mom called. "We left your desserts on the table. Go help yourselves while people are coming in."

The three sat down to fancy dishes of baked banana pudding, piled high with whipped cream. "Yum! I donnae believe I've ever tasted anythin' this good!" Rory said. They ate every bite and finished off the tall glasses of milk they were served. When they heard the music start, they hurried into the next room and found seats just in time. After a few songs, Kris opened with a prayer and read this verse to them:

"What, then, shall we say in response to these things? If God is for us, who can be against us?" —he paused— "This verse comes from the book of Romans, chapter eight, verse thirty-one." He went on to explain what the verse meant. But Rory's mind wandered.

Oh, there've been lots of people against me! The gangs, the authorities and the pirates! But back then, I was nae even thinkin' of God. Was He for me, even so?

Kris continued. "God gave us His one and only son. His best, the one who meant the most to Him. Because of this, we know He will give us all the things we need. He provides us with faith enough to join our lives with His." Kris swallowed, his voice a bit gravely. "And if He never gave us anything else, I believe the gift of salvation would be enough! But He doesn't stop there. He blesses us with so many things." Kris paused again and glanced around the room, his eyes stopping on Ailsa who seemed entranced.

"Ailsa, would you mind sharing something you are thankful to God for?"

"Jist one thin'? I'm nae sure I can narrow it down to one, but off the top of my head, I'd say the beasties. We have such beautiful ones on this island. And the sunsets! I lovvvvve the sunsets, and the sea!"

They all laughed. She *wasn't* able to say just one.

Kris finished by saying, "I want to challenge all of you to take the time tomorrow, as you explore and enjoy the island, to thank God for what He gives us each day. We take so much for granted so much of the time."

"Excuse me, sir." Rory said, raising his hand. "May I say one thin' I'm thankful for?"

"Of course! Go ahead."

"I'm thankful I found this island! My life was a mess before I came 'ere and I didnae 'ave much to look forward to. But ever since I got 'ere, thin's have been lookin' up!"

"I'm thankful for holiday time!" A guest called out. Many guests clapped and agreed. "Aye, holiday time is the best!"

And the rest of the devotional time was spent with people calling out all the things they were thankful for. Kris ended with a prayer of thanksgiving for the greatest gift of all, Jesus, and then they sang one more song. Afterwards, they lingered in the parlor chatting and laughing.

Rory's own heart grew thankful.

The light of thankfulness pushed away the darkness in his life and fed the hope within him. Many of the fears he'd had as he entered the room disappeared, a direct result of thankfulness and meditating on scriptures.

He agreed then that *God is for us! For me!* Then another thought snuck in, *Maybe I have been chosen*.

CHAPTER 14

A NEW THING

Socorro threw a couple of cushions on the floor in front of the fireplace in his room. Rory cradled the wee pup he had chosen, as he lowered himself onto one of them. Socorro hopped on the other. He purposely hadn't invited Ailsa this time. It was a time for just the guys. He tossed Rory an apple and helped himself to another. They were set.

Rory stroked the sleepy pup in his lap. She was a wee girl, brindle in color. He'd never seen one like it! And she had such a sweet temperament. He loved her already. *Could this pup really be mine soon?* He was daydreaming and didn't hear Socorro's last few words.

"Oh, sorry, pal. Pup distracted me. Wha'd, ya say?"

"Hey, no problem. I said, where did you say you lived, before here, I mean."

"I lived in Liverpool, a city in the UK if you're not familiar. I was born there, but the last year or so, life was nae gud. I had me freedom, but it came with a price. There was no place where I felt safe. If I found a half-way decent spot to sleep in, I'd have to sleep with one eye open."

"Oh yeah? Not good at all." Socorro said.

"And it was usually cold and wet. I slept on cardboard and covered meself with old rags. During the day I did me best to stay clear of most of ta' others on the street. Life dealt them all a bad hand and they were mad at the world. Many drank too much or took drugs. But not me! I wanted me wits aboot me! Plus, me da' taught me better.

'Drugs will kill ya,' he said, 'if not physically, they'll kill ya slowly in your spirit.'

He was a smart man, me da'. But findin' a job was impossible. If you're a street person, no one trusts ya." he continued, growing thoughtful as he spoke. "I though' I was lucky when I heard about this fishing boat, a tramp steamer that was hirin'. So, I cleaned meself up and went down to the docks. The boss didnae even ask where I come from, jist hired me on the spot. Later, I found out why!"

"Yeah, I remember you saying it was a bad deal. I'm glad ya got off that steamer. Do ya think any of them will ever come looking for you?"

"I hope nae! But tha's me biggest fear. Ever since Da' died, I found meself in one trouble after another and many times it werenae any fault of me own." Rory looked down at the pup. She was sleeping soundly on his lap. He thought it was best to change the subject so as not to stay in this dark moment. "Wha' aboot you? Tell me how ya got to the island and such."

"Well, It's a pretty long story. Let me see if I can sum it up. My sister, Kristal and I, got lost on a mountain during a camping trip. Our folks completely disappeared after an earthquake hit. We were lost. We thought they were dead! We were on our own then, and let me tell ya, some very mysterious things happened! We were only able to survive it all by our own wits and lots of help from God!"

"Wow!" Rory commented.

"He was not a part of my life before, but I found Him on that mountain. Lots of stuff happened, good and bad. When we finally found our parents, we had no way to get home. We'd even lost our car! After more struggles that included a fight for our lives, we were able to get back home, but in a miraculous way! It was amazing!"

Rory smiled. "But how did ya get here?"

"Well, let me tell ya. life was humdrum after that until one day, Mom got a letter saying she inherited a castle! We all laughed. We thought it was a scam or trick or something. But it wasn't! We flew here to Scotland just to see. Well, it all checked out to be true and the rest is history, as they say."

"Wow! Hard to believe, eh, unless ya believe in miracles! Kinda like me landin' here. Do ya think there's something magic about this place?" Rory asked.

"Well, if ya mean special, I'd say yes! You've seen the coos and Deemer. And talked with them! Not the first talking animals I've encountered. The first time I spoke with a beaver on the mountain, I was sure I'd lost my marbles!" they both laughed.

"I know that feeling." Rory agreed.

"The creatures here don't talk to everyone, really only with us three kids. Kristal and Hamish know about them, but they haven't really talked to them like we have."

"I wonder why?" Rory asked.

Socorro shrugged. "Who knows. But there are many other special animals on the island. Last year, we were able to make friends with a lot of sea creatures and a snowy owl who raised her chicks in the lighthouse."

"Yeah, and I'd say it's pretty special to have this big ole castle to live in!" Rory said.

"For sure. Hey, which room did you end up with? I haven't heard where mom put ya." Socorro asked.

"Wanna see it?" Rory asked. "I'll put the pup up and show ya."

When the puppy was back with its mum, the boys walked to a suite a few rooms down. The number said 333. "Oh, wow you got the VIP suite!" Socorro called out excitedly.

"Yeah, for noo. Tha' was all they had available at the time. Your mum says she'll get me a more permanent room, soon. I'm almost afraid to touch anythin' in this one!" he laughed.

The boys entered the room and sat on the edge of the bed. "Talk aboot a contrast! From the streets of Liverpool to the dignitary suite in a grand Scottish castle!" Rory said as he swept his arm in a gesture of showing off the room.

Socorro laughed. "Yeah, I think God has a cool sense of humor! I was the same way when we first got here. I came from a regular home to all of this!"

An idea popped into Socorro's head. "Hey, how would you feel about staying next door to me? Kristal's talked about getting another room for a while, and since she is gone most of the time, you could have her room. Let's ask!"

"Sounds gud to me, if you donnae think your sister will think we're kickin' her out of her own room!"

"Really, I think it will be fine. She's taking decorating courses, so she loves fixing up rooms. There's still lots of them sitting empty."

"Oh, I see."

"Yes, this floor is just for our family. There's still lots of empty bedrooms." Socorro reassured him. "This fancy suite has never been used before but was set up just in case someone famous visits. Guess that makes you pretty special!" Socorro strolled around the massive space. It was much like the apartment his grandparents lived in with a fancy kitchen, sitting area and massive bedroom.

"Hey, you want to stay in Kristal's room tonight? This place is so big and spooky. I'll ask Mom to make sure it's okay, but what do ya think?"

"Sure, I'd like that! I've really felt out of place here, like I'm pretendin' to be somebody else!"

The boys went downstairs and talked it over with Socorro's parents. They had no objections to the move. They thought it best though, to talk it over with Kristal before they promised to make it permanent.

The boys gathered up Rory's things and moved them to Kristal's room. It didn't take long, since Rory didn't have much.

"Kristal's room is clean, since the maids work on it each Monday after she leaves. So, make yourself at home." Socorro said. "I'll go through my closet and get you a few more things to wear until your own stuff can be ordered."

"Alright, ta!"

"Wait! Rory," Socorro said as he stepped into his room. "Dad asked me to give you this. It's an extra Bible we ordered to be used in the devotional area. It even has extra study guides you might find helpful."

Rory took the Bible. It was thick and heavy with a smooth leather binding. "Wow! I'll take good care of it. When do you need it back?" he asked.

"We don't. It's yours if you want it. We have more." Socorro smiled.

"Wow, tha's the coolest gift I've ever gotten." But as he said it, his heart tightened. Did he really believe he was going to live here with these people and learn to be posh? It was too good to be true. Nothing like this had ever happened to him. *Better nae get too comfortable, Rory*, he reminded himself. It was so easy for fear and doubts to resurface.

"Night, Rory. See you in the morning. Breakfast is at half past seven, so guess we'd better not stay up too late." Socorro reminded him.

"Okay, Socorro, see ya in the morn'."

But the big new Bible was fascinating. He thumbed through it, first studying all the maps. He saw the dividing page of the new and old testaments and ran his hand over the smooth sheet. He turned a few pages and read some of the red letters. He read and read. He flipped back to the

Old Testament and read some there. As he climbed into the big comfy bed, words he found in the book of Isaiah ran through his mind:

> See, I am doing a new thing! Now it springs up; do you not perceive it? I am making a way in the wilderness and streams in the wasteland.
>
> Isaiah 43:19

He didn't understand everything he read, but it certainly seemed like God was doing a new thing in his life. His life had been like a wasteland, and now being here with these folks was like sitting by cool streams. He swallowed down his fears and prayed this would last. And for safety's sake, he prayed for protection against any evil. Especially from those pirates!

CHAPTER 15

THE NIGHTMARE

Rory flew to a sitting position in bed. He gasped for air and his heart galloped. *Where am I?* Despite the warmth of the room, he was chilled to his toes! He shook his head and wiped his face with his hands. What a terrible dream he'd had! He looked around him and finally remembered he was in Kristal's room, in the castle. He breathed in and out slowly to calm himself. He reminded his poor alarmed mind he was safe. At least for now. He shook his head as the details of the dream rushed into his mind.

The loud, raucous voices of the pirates spewing boos and curses sounded all around him. The wind blew his hair into his face, and he shivered in the cold. He was on a narrow plank, his arms tied behind him. The dark water of the sea swirled below him and the scarred face of the captain of the tramp steamer leered at him from behind, causing his blood to freeze. He was forced forward by something sharp biting at his back. He trepidatiously made it to the end of the slimy plank, the wind and sea stinging his skin. The dark, hungry, sea beckoned to him, urging him to jump, when suddenly, he gazed into two red glowing eyes, glaring at him from the water! He jumped!

He jumped alright, but fortunately it was from the mattress to a sitting position. Just a bad dream. What was it Ailsa said she saw behind the door?

Red glowing eyes! He gulped and puffed. Fortunately, he hadn't called out or awakened anyone. He got up and cautiously opened the heavy drapes.

The moon was an enormous yellow ball, reflecting in the waves past the cliffs. He stood there for the longest time, looking out at the heavens.

God, I see your handiwork! How beautiful and calm the night is. Thank ya! You've saved me from the tramp steamer and the evil ones aboard. You've saved me from the streets of Liverpool and the evil there. You've saved me to follow Jesus. How can all this happen in a matter of days? He sat back down on the edge of the bed. *And Lord, I want all ya have for me. I want to learn more and more aboot ya. Please teach me! I can never thank ya enough.*

He flipped on the bedside lamp and picked up the thick Bible he was given. It fell open to the middle. *Psalms.* Should he start here? He wasn't sure. Then he closed it and reopened it at the beginning. He scrolled through the introductory pages until he got to the first page of the text, *Genesis*. "In the beginning God created the heavens and the earth." *I should start here, in the beginning*. He read on.

"Hey, Rory, you up yet?" Socorro called out as he knocked on the door between the rooms.

"Yes, come in." Rory was almost through the book of *Genesis* and didn't want to stop!

"Oh, sorry, I didn't mean to interrupt your morning devotions. What are you reading?"

Rory finished the chapter and looked up. "I'm reading Genesis. Jist finished it actually! God created and created! And the story of Joseph, can you believe it? How he forgave his brothers is beyond me! If the whole Bible is like this, I may never put it down!"

Socorro laughed. "You're new to all of it, right? I've been studying it in our Bible classes, and I'm still finding new and interesting things. It has lots more awesome stories!"

"All true, right?" Rory asked.

"For sure! It's God's word, and it's all true from top to bottom. One of the things we, meaning our family, learned on *Mystic Mountain*, was that God would never lead us astray. We sometimes go astray on our own, like Ailsa's wee sheep, but you'll find that Jesus is the good shepherd. He leads us back to the right path."

"Awesome! I want to stay on the right path. I've seen the other paths and felt the pain and evil. I neva wanna go back!" Rory closed the Bible and set it aside. "Guess it's almost time for breakfast."

"We have about half an hour. Just enough time for us to shower and get dressed. You want to shower first?" Socorro invited.

"Sure, I'll get goin' so you can have your turn." Rory said, pulling out a set of clothes that he was given.

The boys landed at the breakfast table just before the blessing. Ailsa had saved them seats next to her, so the three could discuss plans for the day. Morning classes were on schedule to resume today. But before they got a chance, plans were made for them.

"Rory, I am certainly not going to tell you what to do, but if I might suggest...well, I thought you could study with Socorro. He starts out with Bible classes and then goes on to his other studies which might be helpful to you. Then when the tutor arrives on Friday, we'll get you set up with your own study schedule. What do you say?" Kris asked.

Rory paused to consider it. "Well, sounds like a better plan than I have for the rest of the week, since I have none!" he laughed.

"And about the room," Adara said, "I called Kristal, and she loves the idea of switching rooms. She has some decorating assignments due and thought she could design her own room for credit. So that will leave her present room open for you. I know it's decorated for a girl right now, but once she comes and gets her things moved over, we'll let you pick your own style.

It'll be fun getting everyone settled in their new rooms." Adara smiled at him. She was as excited as Kristal when it came to decorating. Since they had already planned on expanding the number of rooms open to guests, she had a boatload of linen and other decor to use. There would be many options to choose from.

"Yes, ta. It's all brilliant." Rory said as he finished the last bits of his pastry.

Ailsa cleared her plate, silverware and glass to the sink. Everyone pushed back and did likewise. There were chores to be done before classes. The three left the kitchen through the back and entered the sheep enclosure.

Rory greeted the wee animals in the large barn as the other two fed and watered them. He squatted down and rubbed his cheeks on their soft furry heads. They were such fun creatures to play with! They pushed and shoved each other as they sought Rory's attention.

Ailsa stooped down and looked Flumpy in the face. "Oh, my wee lamb! I wonder why you donnae talk to me! So many of the other beasties on the island have thin's to say!" She tousled the wool on his head and rubbed his ears. The lamb just bleated out, "baaaaa!" Ailsa laughed. "You are talkin' to me, aye! I pretty much know wha' yous want, food, water and us to rub ya!" They all laughed.

The kids returned to the kitchen and washed their hands in the service sink. Mary announced that Gee's food was ready to be delivered to him. They grabbed the bags of warm food and raced off to the lighthouse to deliver it.

"Oh wha' a beautiful mornin', oh wha' a beautiful day!" Ailsa sang in her clear voice. The sound rang out across the quiet island and pushed the last remnants of the silent night away. The sun was rising over the sea, and

Rory almost crashed his four-wheeler on a boulder watching it. *I'll never take anything' for granted again, God. Your nature cries out to me soul!*

As the kids delivered the food inside the lighthouse, Rory removed his helmet and listened to the sound of the sea. Gentle waves rolled onto the beach leaving white foam and wet sand in their wake. He smelled the fishy air and tasted the salty mist. He loved the sea and decided he could never get enough of it. The others came out laughing, startling him from his meditation.

They mounted the bikes and raced off up the beach like he had seen them do last week. Had it only been a week since he landed on this island? What a difference there was in his life, already. He let out a whoop as he followed them, gulping in the fresh crisp air.

They pulled up close to the rocky crag and cut the engines. Off came their shoes and socks. They raced along the beach enjoying the feel of the sand in their toes. Ailsa shrieked as the frigid water swept over her feet, then veered out of the way of the approaching tide. They laughed and frolicked for a bit, their cheeks rosy red.

"Ark, ark, ark," the seals barked as they splashed nearby. They seemed to be laughing at the kids as they tossed their slick heads out of the water.

"Whew, that was fun!" Socorro panted, catching his breath. "But we gotta go!"

"Too bad we have to leave," Rory spoke what they all were feeling.

Reluctantly, they donned their footwear and headed back. He hoped this would be their morning routine forever!

CHAPTER 16

THE BLAZING FURNACE

Ailsa pulled into the garage. But her mind was elsewhere, thinking about that mysterious door and what was behind it. Hearing the noise of the workmen sawing wood and shooting nails, gave her an idea! There were unending projects around the massive old castle, but today, the noise seemed to be coming from the garden.

I'll ask the workmen if they can open the door we found, so we can explore! She hurried over to the garden and found them.

Oooh, they're building a gazebo! She clapped her hands. The structure was still in its beginning stages, but judging from what she could see, it was going to be a tall semi-round structure with steps and wooden seats. *What a neat place it will be to hang out in when they get it done*, she thought.

"S'cuse me. May I ask a question?" she asked one of the blokes who had paused in his work. She smiled and used all her charm. "There's a broken door upstairs. Can anyone get it open for me?"

The workman sighed. He looked at the young girl and answered. "Aye, we can, but your da' needs to bring us a work order. Nae sure when we can get to it, though. We have a stack of work orders as high as the roof already, so if its urgent, he needs to mark it as such." The man turned and went back to work.

Ailsa frowned. *Well, tha' didnae go well!* she thought. There must be another way to get the door open. She wasn't going to ask Mr. Frazier for a work order!

The older lads were already in the library. "I'm not sure where Ailsa went, but she'll be here soon. She's never late for class. I'm the one who drags my feet getting here." Socorro laughed.

As he spoke, Ailsa appeared at the door. "Hey, Wha' are we goin' to do to get tha' door open? It's been buggin' me since yesterday!"

"I've no clue. But you know we have to get our work done before we can go check it out again. So, let's hurry and finish as fast as we can!" Socorro suggested.

Rory was perusing the many books on the shelves. He was hoping to find something light to read while the others studied. He finally chose a book about the history of the island. It wouldn't hurt to learn about the place where he lived. He sat crossed legged on the floor near the fireplace.

"We usually open our devotionals and read, say a prayer and then get started. Want to join us?" Ailsa asked.

Rory shrugged. "Sure, why nae?"

"The thought for today is 'Would you choose the fire?'" Ailsa read. "It's not a thought anyone would want to consider, but in Daniel chapter three, three teenage boys had to make that decision. King Neb-a-ca-nez-er, or somethin' like tha'," she started.

"I think it's Neba-ka-nez-zar," Socorro piped in.

"Well, anyway, the King had a golden figure set up and he called all the officials to the dedication and said they must bow down to it. The herald proclaimed, 'All you people, as soon as you hear the instruments start to play, and you hear the music, you must fall down and worship this image of gold, or you will be thrown into the blazing furnace!'"

Rory sat mesmerized!

"All the people and nations fell down and worshiped the golden figure. Except, three young Jewish boys, named Shadrach, Meshach and Abednego!" Ailsa continued. "An astrologer came up and informed the King that the boys would not worship the image as commanded. The King was furious! He called the boys to appear before him and asked them if it was true that they would not bow down to the gods of the King and to the golden image!"

"It was true!" Socorro said, remembering the story he'd heard in the past.

"The King told them that when they heard the music, they were to fall down and worship the image! But, if you donnae, then into the furnace ya go! Then what god would rescue you?"

"The lads answered him and said, "If we are thrown into the blazing furnace, the God we serve will save us. But even if he doesnae, we will not serve your gods or the image of gold you set up."

"The King threw them in!" Socorro shouted dramatically.

"Hey, I was still readin'" Ailsa reminded him.

"So, they tied the boys up, fully clothed and threw them in! The furnace was so blazin' hot; it killed the soldiers who threw them in—" She stopped and took a drink from her water bottle.

"Well, donnae leave us hangin'" Rory coaxed.

"King Nebuchadnezzar jumped up and said, 'Hey weren't there three men thrown in?'"

They said, "Yes, your majesty."

"The king shouted, 'Look, I see four men walking around in the fire and the fourth looks like a son of the gods!'"

"Who was it?" Rory asked. "It must have been a god, because who else can walk in fire?" he mused.

"It was Jesus, he was right there with 'em." Socorro said.

"Or maybe an angel. It doesn't say. But we know God saved them." Ailsa said.

Rory's eyes grew large, and the hair rose up on his arms. "Then wha'?"

"The King called them by name, 'Shadrach, Meshach and Abednego, come out!' So, they did! And nae one bit of clothing was burned, nae one hair on their heads was burned and they didnae even smell like smoke!" she said excitedly!

"And because of what the King saw, he made all the kingdom worship the God of Shadrach, Meshach and Abednego or be cut up into pieces! He even gave the three lads a promotion."

Rory sat there, thinking about the story. "Would I be brave enough to go in the fire? I want tha' much faith!" he told the others.

"I get it," Socorro said. "I didn't have much faith, but I learned on *Mystic Mountain* that God was there for me no matter what, even in the worst situations, like being captured by a dragon! But even if we don't have to prove our love for Him by being in a furnace, there's plenty of other ways to show it!"

The kids stopped and joined hands for prayer time. They thanked God for always being there for them, no matter what. And they prayed to please Him in their thoughts, words and deeds.

After the prayer, they took out their tablets and got started on the assignments set up for them. Rory noticed he had already finished the lessons Socorro was working on, so he went to his room and retrieved the Bible he was given and spent time reading more of Daniel. *Who knew the Bible had such exciting stories?* he thought.

The morning proved to be productive and thankfully, they were able to complete the assignments before lunch. Now they could have some fun!

CHAPTER 17

THE FUNNY HAT

After lunch Kris found the boys and said, "Hey guys, my shipment has come in, and I could use some help. How about you come with me to pick up some things from the dock? You've finished your studies for the day, Socorro?"

"Actually, I have, believe it or not! I wanted to finish early so we could have the rest of the day free. What are you getting, Dad?"

"We're picking up food supplies and such. But I could use a bit of muscle to get it all loaded and unloaded. It looks like fresh fish might be on the menu, too. There is a tramp steamer docked and they're advertising fresh fish for sell."

Rory gulped. *There's no way it could be 'my' tramp steamer, could it? Not very likely since I left it over a week ago. They must be miles away by now. But still, what if?*

"So, what do ya say, Rory, mind helping out for a few hours? There will be pay at the end. I don't expect my workers to work for free!" Kris smiled.

Rory answered, "I donnae mind helpin', but instead of pay, I was wondering if I might 'ave one of those pups when they are weaned. Fosters pups, I mean. I'll work off however much it is to buy her."

Kris laughed. "Sure, no problem. We have a lot of them to get rid of. If you're willing to care for it, you're welcome to have one. But we don't expect you to pay since we're going to give them away, anyway."

Rory grinned. "I neva had a pet! And I 'ave already got one picked ou'. The little brindle one. I am going to call her Brandi Brindle!" he laughed.

Kris chuckled. "Sounds good. I like the name, too. I'm glad you brought this up, because while we're in the village, we need to see if anyone else is interested in adopting a pup. It won't be long until they are ready, and nine dogs is a bit much to have loose in the castle."

"Mr. Frazier, may I tag along, too? I'd like to help." Ailsa volunteered.

"Sure, Ailsa, check with your mum and if it's alright, you're welcome to come too."

She nodded, and a crease formed in her brow. *If I don't watch out, I'm going to be left out since Socorro has a new pal!* she frowned.

It was unusually busy at the dock yard. Several big ships were waiting in the queue to unload. An overloaded barge was first in the line and was ready to land at the dock.

Ailsa jumped from the truck and ran to a roped-off area. There were about a dozen pelicans hanging out there, and she wanted to see them.

As she approached, they called out nosily as they swooped to scoop up fish along the bay wall.

She stood still watching them, when suddenly one of the large billed, winged creatures landed on her head! His webbed feet slipped around on her curls, as he flapped his wings for balance. The enormous bird who was over half her size, was almost too much for the wee lass! But she stood as still as a post, her neck shaking under the weight of it. But then she began to giggle! And as she giggled, her entire body shook. But the ole' bird was not deterred. He just sat there making himself comfortable!

Socorro, watching the whole thing, laughed hysterically. He reached in his pocket and pulled out his phone and snapped a couple of photos! Both boys teased her mercilessly.

"Nice hat ya got on!" Socorro shouted.

"Hope she doesnae make a nest in your hair!" Rory shouted, laughing.

"Okay, you guys. The barge is coming in, and I need you to be ready." Kris said, smiling. It *was* pretty hilarious!

Ailsa shooed the bird away and ran over. Once the ship was secured to the post, they formed an assembly line. Ailsa was paired with Kris, then the boxes were handed from one to the next, then to the next, until the truck was loaded and ready to go.

The freight barge moved away and opened up the slot for the next waiting vessel. Rory froze when he saw the tramp steamer docking. *It was the one he had escaped from!* He ran to the truck and ducked behind it. His heart raced in his chest, making it hard to think of his next move. He stealthily opened the door of the vehicle and snuck in, staying low on the floorboards.

Socorro noticed him disappear in haste and decided to find out what was going on. He went around the truck and opened the door. "What are ya doing? Hiding?"

Rory held a finger to his lips in a "shhh" signal and waved him in. Socorro crouched near him.

Rory spoke rapidly, "The tramp steamer tha's pullin' into the dock is the one I escaped from! I'm afraid they'll see me! It's full of evil men doin' evil things. Please, tell your da' that we must leave noo!"

Socorro rushed back to his dad who was lugging a big basket of fish. "Grab a handle and help me with this, son."

Socorro helped him get over to the truck and tied it down.

"Dad, we need to get out of here!" he said under his breath. "Rory says that tramp steamer is full of bad guys and is the one he escaped from!"

Kris turned and looked at the fishing boat. Other than it being weathered and in need of repair, there was nothing unusual about it. The workers continued to off-load fish. "Let me see what I can find out. You kids stay in the truck."

Socorro signaled for Ailsa, and they both squeezed in around Rory, who was still on the floor.

"Wha's goin' on?" Ailsa asked loudly.

"Shhh!" Rory shrank lower, pressing himself flat on the floor, avoiding their muddy feet.

"Jist sit still and look forward. And lock the doors!"

Rory, who seemed scared out of his wits, convinced them that there was danger, so they did as he asked. After a long fifteen minutes, Kris returned to the truck with another full basket of fish. He loaded it in the back then used the remote to open the door to the driver's side and got in.

"I had a look around and got the boats name. *Sea Witch*. I'll have some friends of mine from the M.C.A. check it out. If there is illegal stuff going on, they'll get to the bottom of it. Just stay down, Rory, and we'll get out of here."

Kris turned the truck around and headed toward the village. He braked and pulled into the parking area of the grocery store on the island. "You guys sit tight; I have a few more things to pick up before we head back. Do you think anyone saw you, Rory?"

"I donnae think so. I skedaddled when I saw the boat! But I cannae be certain." He shivered. "Please, hurry. If those blokes find me, I'm done for!"

Socorro and Ailsa kept watch as Dad finished his errands. Nothing unusual happened except a woman walking a dog meandered by.

"I hope he hurries; me legs are crampin'!" Rory whined.

It wasn't long after that, Kris came out carrying a large bag. He rummaged around in it and brought out cold sodas, handing them back to each kid. "I hope you like orange soda. There's not much variety in the store, but this will keep you from dying of thirst." He opened his own soda, took a long swig of it, then threw the truck into reverse and backed out.

Rory stayed on the floor, hoping to shirk detection. It was so weird to see the *Sea Witch* in the bay! He had hoped he would never see it again! Now he would be forced to look over his shoulder day and night, watching for the sleazy blokes who were after him! He sat up enough to take a long draw from the soda bottle as they bounced along on the rough road.

"Maybe ya should change your appearance a bit, like dye your hair or cut it in a different style." Ailsa said. "We'll help ya! We'll get Kristal to bring home hair dye from the city and Adara can cut your hair."

"Might nae be a bad idea! Should I get a color like yours? We cud be twins!" Rory grinned.

Ailsa laughed. "A tall bloke like you and a wee girl like me, twins?" The thought was quite comical.

"Well, if it makes you feel more comfortable, I think you *should* change your appearance. It's better to be careful. And I don't want you scared all the time. We'll get to the bottom of this with the M.C.A., but change your hair, if you want." Kris said, as he parked the truck in the garage.

They unloaded the supplies from the truck and stacked them on the kitchen floor. They handed the baskets of fish over to Mary and she and the other kitchen staff began cleaning and preparing them for the freezer. Then Kris took one of the cartons and went into the parlor. "Hey, come over here and see what I got for you guys," he called to them. "You'll need something to keep you busy during the long winter months ahead. Open it up!"

The kids dove into the carton. They pulled out several gigantic sets of plastic building blocks! One of them was a kit to build the *Titanic*, and the other two were elaborate Christmas village scenes.

"Lights are included!" Kris informed them.

"Ta! I love it Mr. Frazier," Ailsa said, giving Kris a quick hug.

"Yes! I've neva' had the opportunity to build any of those sets, but I've always wanted to." Rory said, intrigued.

"Good. Take them to the library. After all your hard work, you deserve some down time. I'll be sure to pay you all after supper."

The kids beamed at each other. It had been a good day, except for the tramp steamer situation! But Rory felt safe now, back in the big castle. After all, it was fortified and built to protect those within.

He pushed all thoughts of danger out of his mind. He was anxious to get started on the building sets. They each grabbed one and headed upstairs.

CHAPTER 18

Behind the Door

The kids kept busy and finished out the week, applying themselves to the required study assignments. When there was free time, they kept busy with the elaborate building blocks. They'd set them up in the library on different tables and worked on them between courses. Rory worked on the *Titanic*, and the others worked on the Christmas villages. When they tired of the building blocks, they had fun dramatizing the Bible stories they read each day. Sometimes they'd dress up in costumes made from blankets and curtain tie backs. It helped make the Bible come alive!

Though the days were quite frigid, Rory took his pup out during the warmest part of the day. He played with her as much as he dared keep her away from her mum. Only one more week and he could take sweet Brandi Brindle away from the litter. He planned to let her sleep in his room, maybe even in his bed if she wanted to cuddle.

The days passed quickly and the weekend snuck up on them. Hamish and Kristal were home on holiday the entire week! It was Autumn break at the University. In fact, they were all on holiday, no studies for a week! When the tutor came by, she told Rory she would wait to test him until after the break. That was fine by him!

Ailsa and her mum left for the weekend as Kristal and Hamish arrived, as was the usual routine.

The past few days had gone by fast and there hadn't been a spare moment to check out the mysterious door, or the glowing eyes. In fact, that door and the mysteries it held had been completely forgotten. But before they could say 'what happened', they found that the weekend was over and Ailsa was back.

The family found it was busier than ever during the break. By request from Rory, Kristal brought a hair dye kit home from the city and helped him change his hair color. Afterwards, Adara cut and styled it to a shorter, funkier, cut. They patterned it after a style they found online that was entirely different than his usual hair style.

He said goodbye to his shoulder-length hair and welcomed the short trendy cut. His honey-blond locks were transformed into dark brown, and with the new hair style, Rory was a different bloke!

And that wasn't the only change happening. The castle was in a state of transformation. They all pitched in and decorated it for the upcoming autumn festival. The village, too, was going all out with elaborate decorations, getting ready for the annual parade. Being adept in design, Kristal led the endeavor, at least where the castle was concerned.

The cartons they had recently hauled home, not only held food, but were loaded with supplies for the holiday. They used the parlor area and entry as headquarters. The tables were piled high with craft supplies to make the decorations. Pumpkins were brought in from the garden as well as baskets filled with gourds, corn and berries. Strings of lights and wrapped candy were spread out everywhere.

Ailsa came into the room and saw Hamish. He was gingerly surveying the massive amounts of decor spread out in the area. It gave her an idea! Hamish was a handyman before he went off to Uni and knew the castle pretty well. Maybe he could help open the handle-less door!

"Hamish! Can you give me a hand?" she asked.

"Maybe, wha's up?"

"Come upstairs and let me show ya. I cannae open a door because there's no knob," she explained as she started up the stairs.

Hamish grabbed a handful of the candy on the table and followed her. He munched a few treats on the way up. At the top, Ailsa stopped on the landing. She felt nervous. *What if a dangerous animal charges out?* She turned and looked Hamish in the eyes since he was standing on a lower step and was level with her height. "Wait! Maybe this isnae a gud idea! Last time I was up here, I saw scary red eyes through the hole in the door. I donae want ya to be hurt! What should we do?" She twisted her hands restlessly.

Hamish swallowed his last bite of candy and smiled at her. "Scary red eyes! Aye, I think we can defeat that monster!" He squeezed past Ailsa and looked in the hole where the doorknob should have been.

"Wha's there? See anything?" she inquired.

Hamish took out his phone and activated the flashlight. He then peered in again. It looked like a dusty alcove in the tower. He didn't see much else, but his visibility was limited. He reached in the hole and around the facing. He found the lever that allowed the door to open. It let out a loud creak as it swung inward.

Ailsa stepped back and covered her mouth with her hand. No way was she going in there until he said the coast was clear!

Hamish pushed the door open wider to allow in more light. Cobwebs were thick in the corridor, and he brushed them aside. Toward the back, there was another wee door, wooden with a golden knob. He crossed the room and tried the doorknob, but it was locked. He activated the flashlight again and called Ailsa. "Come on in, there's nothin' to be afraid of. Just an old dusty passageway."

"I'm sure I saw wolf eyes last time!" —she stepped in cautiously— "Bbbbut there's no windows are there, jist that wee door in the back. How odd."

"Aye it's locked. Probably nothin' but an old storage area." He turned back to exit the musty room. "I bet it was the way the light caused shadows on the wall tha' scared ya. There's nothing here." He flipped off his phone light and exited the room.

Ailsa sneezed, then followed him out. "Jist dust and cobwebs. I'm sorry, Hamish, I was positive I saw something. Thank ya for coming with me to check it out. Maybe it *was* jist the light." she shrugged.

"Guess we'd better find the others and help with the festival." Hamish said, already descending the stairs.

When they got back to the parlor, Kristal had assigned all of them jobs. Rory, Socorro and Hamish were assigned garden decorating. (The actual labor of putting up the decor, hanging the lights and carrying the heavy stuff, that is). The girls were in charge of directing and decorating the inside.

It was all going fairly smoothly, until the boys got a wee bit confused about where the lights and pumpkins were supposed to go, so Kristal drew out a plan. Hamish laid the blueprint out on one of the tables and did his best to decipher it. He removed his hat and scratched his head. "Socorro, check this ou'. Any idea wha' your sister means here?" He pointed to the paper.

"Nope, not a clue," Socorro said as he studied the pictures. Rory leaned over the table and the three of them studied it. After a length of time and a lot of discussion, Socorro took the paper and wadded it into a ball, then stuck it in his pocket.

Rory laughed, lifted a hefty pumpkin and set it next to a tree trunk. Then Hamish dropped a hay bale nearby and Socorro planted a floppy scarecrow on it!

"There ya go!" Rory cried.

Next, they placed a wheelbarrow on the path and loaded it with straw, then added a cute scarecrow couple to look like they were going for a ride. They surrounded them with several pumpkins. Rory stapled a black crow on the man scarecrow's hat, and called it done.

But they weren't finished yet! Millions of lights were strung from the tree branches! The whole garden was filled with orange bulbs. Then the guys placed wee squirrel figurines all around the garden. Finally, they stopped to admire their handiwork. "Who needs a plan?" they joked.

A huge pile of fallen leaves under one of the trees was too much for Foster. She jumped into them and started rolling and scattering them around. It looked like so much fun, the boys ended up doing the same thing. Before long, they were shouting, laughing and tossing leaves at each other.

Ailsa heard laughter and decided to see what the blokes were up to. Besides, she needed a break. Spreading the fancy cloths on the tables and setting up the centerpiece arrangements was not very fun. Working indoors was boring and she would rather be outdoors with the lads. She slipped on her heavy jacket and skipped to the garden.

"Whoa! I love it!" she giggled as she came through the garden gate. Foster ran up to her and licked her hand. She bent down and removed a few leaves from the dog's long fur and gave her head a pat.

When the lads saw Ailsa, they grinned at each other. Socorro pointed discreetly at the girl, and they all nodded. As Ailsa approached, they grabbed her!

The squealing child was lifted into the air and tossed into the pile of leaves! They laughed so hard, they bent over, holding their guts!

Ailsa pushed herself out and pretended to pout. She grabbed a fist full of leaves and threw it at one of them. The leaves fell to the ground just in front of her, causing another bout of laughter, even Ailsa couldn't help but laugh. Then she brushed herself off and walked through the garden to see their work.

"I donnae how you did all this, but it's brilliant! I bet even Kristal will like it."

"Speaking of Kristal, here she comes." Hamish said, grinning mischievously. He ran over and scooped her up and gently tossed her into the pile of leaves that Ailsa had just exited. Then they all tossed leaves over her until she was completely buried.

"Stop, stop!" she laughed, pushing the leaves away. Foster ran over and started frantically digging into the leaves. Soon, Kristal was free, and the dog was licking her as if she had truly saved her life. Laughing, Kristal pushed her back and got up.

"Well, wha' do ya think?" Hamish asked, his arms outstretched as he twirled around. "We fixed it up noo didnae we?"

Kristal smiled. Although it didn't look much like the plans she had given them, it was festive. She gave Hamish a hug and an approving look. He beamed.

"I cannae wait to see the lights, once it gets dark. But look, let me show you what we did over here." He took her hand and the two wandered off.

"Guess we might as well go in and get some hot apple cider," Socorro laughed. "We'll leave those two love birds to themselves."

Ailsa called Foster over and they headed in, happy to escape the frigid, fall air.

Hamish and Kristal hadn't much 'alone' time lately. When they were home, too many people depended on them to get things done either at the castle or at the lighthouse. So, these few stolen moments were priceless. It couldn't have worked out better for Hamish, and he couldn't let this moment pass! He led her over to the newly built Gazebo, now covered with holiday lights. They sat close together on the bench.

He took her hand and gave it a brief kiss. Then he spoke softly, his lips near her ear, "I know we still have a couple of years left at the Uni, but I think we're at the point in our relationship to be making some important decisions," his forehead wrinkled in a serious expression. "Since we are apart all week and only see each other on weekends and holidays, I want to make it clear to everyone that our hearts belong to each other." he grinned. "I want ya to think on this, my bonnie lass, but can we be somethin' more than jist boyfriend/girlfriend?" Hamish slipped his arm around her.

Kristal's heart did a major flip flop! *What's he going to say?* "But what would we be if we're more than just girlfriend/boyfriend?" she asked, a mischievous smile on her face.

The setting sun was peeking through the tree branches, illuminating her face at just the right angle. *She's downright angelic.* he thought. He licked his lips and his hand shook slightly as he took her left hand and slipped a wee silver ring on her finger. It had a single diamond, just large enough to catch the light and gleam!

Kristal squealed and threw her arms around his neck. "I would never let anyone else get between us! But thank you, it's beautiful," she whispered. Hamish kissed her softly, to seal the deal.

Kristal held her hand up so she could admire the ring in the fading light. She smiled. *Wow! Could this day get any better?*

"This means we are now promised to each other!" He pulled her close and gave her another kiss. He stood up then and offered his hand to help her up. He held her at arm's length so he could look into her eyes. They shone with the depth of caring he was hoping to see! Now *his* heart did a flip flop.

Suddenly the holiday lights came on! The entire garden was lit up! The answer to Kristal's question about the day was *yes, it could get better!* She would remember this day, forever and always!

They heard loud voices laughing and chatting as they headed their way. The moment was over and they quickly let go of each other.

Hamish took her hand as they joined the others and they all headed back to the castle. His heart was full. He hoped the two of them would grow even closer over these next few years until they were able to be married. But the time needed to pass fast, because he was ready to marry her now! But wait they must. He realized that they both must grow up a bit more and also fulfill their proper callings. In other words, they must finish Uni first! *Only two and a half more years*, he told himself. *Three at the most*. With God's help, they could do it!

CHAPTER 19

COUNTING BLESSINGS

That evening, the group gathered around the massive fireplace in the front parlor for devotions. It was only the staff and family tonight. All the guests were occupied elsewhere.

Kristal was floating in dreamland, pondering the last few moments she spent with Hamish in the garden. She still couldn't believe she now wore his ring, the promise ring. She and Hamish sat side by side waiting for the devotion time to start, fingers entwined.

Dad dimmed the overhead lights, and the crackling fire added a cozy, romantic ambiance. Not a sound was heard the first few minutes. Then he stood up and opened them in a prayer of praise and thanksgiving. After the prayer, he asked them a question: "What should we do to seek God?" Not waiting for an answer, he read these words slowly with meaning:

"James 4:8a says, 'Come near to God and he will come near to you.'" he paused then said, "Verse 10 says: 'Humble yourselves before the Lord and he will lift you up.'" Again, he paused, looking at each of them around the room. Then he said, "Once we draw near to God and humble ourselves, meaning giving all the glory to Him, we are lifted up by Him. But He asks us to do a few things. Isaiah 1:17 says, 'Learn to do right: seek justice. Defend the oppressed. Take up the cause of the fatherless; plead the case of the widow.'" Rory held up his hand.

"Yes, Rory." Kris said.

"I'm fatherless, and yous took me in." he said quietly.

Then Adara spoke. "I'm an orphan, too. My mom and dad were killed when I was very young."

"Aye, me too." Hamish said. "Gee cared for me all my life."

Rory's eyes grew large, "Wow, we've got a lot in common, then. Sometimes when you go through bad stuff, you think you're the only one, makes ya feel alone. Thanks, for lettin' me know I'm nae the only one."

"And the Bible has a lot more to say about orphans, because before we meet God, we are all fatherless. Turn in your Bibles to Psalms 146:9." Kris typed rapidly on his tablet until the verses popped up. He waited until they had all found the verse.

"Psalms 146:9 says, 'The Lord watches over the foreigner and sustains the fatherless and the widow, but he frustrates the ways of the wicked.' Now turn to the next verse, Psalm 68:5, which says 'A father to the fatherless, a defender of widows, is God in his holy dwelling.' But that's not all, back in Psalm 27:10, it reminds us that 'Though my father and mother forsake me, the Lord will receive me.' He becomes our Father."

Rory raised his hand again. "Erm, excuse me but...well, I'm thinkin' aboot when I was on the tramp steamer. I thought there was no way out! It's clear ta me noo, though, what God did for me. He helped me escape. He sent the light from the lighthouse at jist the right time and then He helped me be brave enough to jump! He saved me from almost certain death in the sea, and he brought me to yous." He stopped, his eyes growing misty. He swallowed, then said, "And noo, it's becomin' clear to me as I sit through this lesson, wha' He wants me to do! I must learn all I can and share it with those who donnae know, like I didnae know, like the other orphans on the streets of Liverpool."

Adara gasped! *What wise words from this new believer! He really is growing fast in the Lord!*

Kris continued, "Yes, so true Rory. It makes me think of Romans 10:14-15. It says, 'How, then, can they call on the one they have not believed in? And how can they believe in the one of whom they have not heard? And how can they hear without someone preaching to them? And how can anyone preach unless they are sent? As it is written: How beautiful are the feet of those who bring good news!'" Kris looked at Rory. "It sounds like God is sending you, to bring good news to those who are lost. Let's pray for Rory, now." They bowed their heads. "Socorro, will you pray please?" Kris asked.

Socorro stood up and laid his hand on Rory's shoulder. "Dear God, please lead Rory as he seeks to follow you. We know that you can and do use young people, like Rory, and the rest of us kids here. Even though he is new to learning about you, he is listening to Your voice, already, I can tell. So, give him wisdom. Make him brave. In your Holy name, Father. Amen."

Mary stood up then and announced, "There's snacks and tea in the kitchen!" She and the kitchen staff led the way. The group meandered in to enjoy the refreshments, chatting as they gathered.

Adara happened to notice Kristal's ring! She gasped and pulled her daughter aside. "Kristal, you're too young! Is that an engagement ring?"

Kristal reassured her it was just a promise ring. "It just means were not seeing others." Adara hugged her daughter. "It's beautiful, Kristal. You chose a good man to partner with. You plan on finishing your education, right?"

"Of course. Mom. We know we're not ready yet for the responsibilities of marriage."

"I'll be praying for you both." she said as she kissed Kristal's cheek. *My little girl is growing up too fast!* She wiped a stray tear away, before anyone noticed.

Ailsa kept yawning, so her mum suggested she head up to bed. Rory realized that he, too, was exhausted and decided to go to his room as well. Besides, he wanted to think about the things he had learned.

As Kris spoke, Rory had carefully written down each scripture reference to look up again, later. There were so many thoughts running through his head! He was learning more about God each day. God loved him! But not just that, but also about what God wanted him to do next! He felt a burden for all those lads still lost, hungry and without homes. *How can they learn about God without someone telling them?*

Since he knew what it was like to be one of them, they might listen to him! He felt a deep longing inside him to share the good news of Jesus, and what had happened in his life, with others.

He opened the door to his room and the light from the fireplace greeted him, wrapping him in its warmth just as the heavenly Father was wrapping his heart in love. He had no words to describe how he felt. When God speaks to the inner most being of your soul, the emotions are totally indescribable, and this was one of those moments. He ended his day praying and counting his blessings. He jotted them down on his paper.

1. I'm safe and warm.

2. I've been adopted by God, and I'm no longer an orphan, but a part of something big!

3. I'm going to get my pup tomorrow!

His heart leapt. *Me very own pup! I never dreamed of such good things coming to me!*

But his heavy eyelids gave way to exhaustion, and he fell asleep, his paper and pencil slipping out of his hand.

CHAPTER 20

SWEET NEEPS

The wolves circled. Their fiery eyes glowed in the blackness of the night. Their eerie howls traveled, amplified by the brisk wind, that carried their cries across the island. They huddled together and schemed against the powers of the light.

"All is not well, for you." they yipped. "We are not giving up! Traps will be set and when you least expect it, you'll be caught like a mouse after cheese! We will get you, and all the other sheep! We will devour your little flock! Just wait! Yip, Yip, Arooo!" they howled.

The Clydesdales shivered as they heard the eerie calls in the night. They grew restless and stomped their enormous hooves. They weren't in danger, but the sheep were! They galloped off to warn all the beasties, especially the sheep!

Rory flew to a sitting position in bed, his heart racing. The morning light was just beginning to filter through the window. He rubbed his eyes as he began to remember the dream he just had. He had dreamed he was back on the ship, and the crew had cornered him. They were throwing things at him and beating him savagely with ropes! Why was he having these dreams? Last evening was so special and uplifting, so why the nightmares? Was he in danger? He opened his window and gazed out at the sea. In the distance, he heard the melodic singing of a female voice. Or was it voices? He listened carefully.

"Show me your loving face! I'll be your dwelling place, Jesus Divine. Closeness is what I crave, 'tween here and the grave, Savior of mine."

The melody danced through the breeze and gave him chill bumps. He rubbed his arms in an effort to calm the emotion he felt. The song was beautiful and the singers harmonized the chorus perfectly. But wait, what time was it? He glanced at the mantle clock. Yikes, he'd slept in!

He heard water running in the bathroom and figured it was Socorro; he must have slept in too. He impatiently rapped on the door. Socorro stuck his head out, still drying his face on a towel. He yawned and entered Rory's room. "Well, we're late for breakfast! Guess we both slept in! Let's go down and see if there's any food left."

"Yes, and it's too bad I did, I had a nightmare!" Rory told him.

"A nightmare? Tell me about it." He sat down on the overstuffed chair, near the fire. Rory sat on the edge of his bed and shared what he remembered.

"It was about me days back on the ship. I donnae remember all of the details but I was always in danger there and I guess it took a toll on me. It will take time to rid meself of all those memories, I guess." He leaned back on his arms. "What should I do to rid meself of them quicker? Your dad had the tramp steamer checked out, but since the sailors had papers, there wasn't anythin' could be done, he told me." Rory stood up and wandered around the length of the room. He continued. "They always put on a good front. They try to look legit, but behind the scenes, they're pure evil. I keep expectin' them to come for me and kill me for jumpin' ship! And all that fear shows up in me dreams!"

"I get it. When we got back from *Mystic Mountain*, certain things woke me at night! Memories. Evil takes its toll on all of us. But when I was on the mountain, I learned that God was with us through it all. He taught us to be brave and strong! He sent His 'helpers' to guide us and protect us. It wasn't until later I learned they were angels!"

"How did He tell you? To be brave and strong, I mean."

"Well, we read verses in the Bible. There are a lot that talk about how we need to be strong and brave. I'm not great at remembering scriptures but I memorized this one, 'Have I not commanded you? Be strong and courageous. Do not be afraid; do not be discouraged, for the Lord your God will be with you wherever you go.'"

"That's one of my favorite ones, now. It helps me remember how God was with me on the mountain and how He is still with me here on the island. It's a good one for you to remember too. Look it up, Joshua 1:9."

"Right. I'm not that far into the Bible yet. I'm readin' from the beginnin' and tryin' to take it all in. But, yeah, I need that one as a reminder. I'll do my best to memorize it." Rory's stomach growled loudly. "Hey, let's go find some food."

The boys dressed quickly and went to the kitchen.

"Hi, guys. You sleepy heads finally get up?" Adara asked. "We've finished breakfast, but there's some fruit and pastries left."

"Thankfully the lasses were singing, or I would still be upstairs. Sorry to be late." Rory said.

Adara smiled. She knew that getting used to a new routine was probably hard for the lad. He'd adjust.

Socorro took out two glasses and filled them with milk. He gulped his down, drinking nosily. He grabbed an apple and headed out the back door. "Come on, Rory, let's see if the girls are still feeding the sheep."

Rory drank his milk and snagged a cinnamon roll. He followed Socorro out. "Thanks for the food," he called back.

Adara laughed and shook her head. *Teens!* As the boys ran out, they stopped to listen to the sweet song dancing on the breeze.

I hear Your voice as the wee bird tweets,
and taste Your love in the air so sweet.
I feel Your breath on the warm, south
wind, the blessings from You have no
end!
The field of wildflowers cries out Your
name, as the sea, the mountains and
the sunsets flame! The orange, the
green, the lavender, the smells! Oh!
What a love Your nature dispels!

"Great harmonizing!" Socorro yelled as he came up. Both girls jumped! The wee sheep dashed toward him and nearly knocked him down.

"Ta, something I wrote recently." Ailsa answered.

"Wow!" Rory exclaimed. "You have a gift!"

"Ta, that's kind of ya. Jist praising the Lord this beautiful mornin'! And the sheep seem to like it."

"Hey, I see you guys finally got up!" Kristal teased. "What do you have planned for today?"

"Not sure. Probably helping to get ready for the festival. When does it start?"

"It starts Friday night, around suppertime, I think." Ailsa piped in. "We're going to see if we can get one of these sheep to pull a cart! For the parade!"

"That seems like a tough thing to accomplish!" Rory laughed. "And what will she have in her cart?"

"Puppies!" they both called out.

"Nope, not my pup!" Rory shook his head. "The cart is sure to turn over, and all the pups will fall out. Better think of another plan."

Kristal laughed, "Yeah, well, it was just an idea. We're actually going to do some decorating and room changing! Right, Ailsa?"

"Aye, Kristal and I decided to share a room. Since she is gone during the week, and I'm gone during the weekend, we will barely see each other. It will be like having rooms of our own, but sharing too. Kristal can decorate so well, I know it will be beautiful! And our room is so much closer to you guys, so watch out." She giggled, pushing her glasses up on her nose. "Want to see it when we're done?"

"Sure..." Socorro said, eyeing Rory. He wasn't really interested but saying so would be rude.

"But right now, we're going to visit the coos. We haven't been there in a while, and they'll be wondering if we have forgotten them. Rory, let's see if there are any veggie scraps around."

"Say Hi to them for me!" Ailsa called. The girls had finished feeding the sheep, so they headed up to work in the bedroom.

Socorro rummaged through the bin and found scraps of cabbage, carrots and turnips. He put it all in a wee pail he'd used before for such outings. Then he let his mom know they would be back by lunchtime. Since they were late for breakfast, he promised they'd be back on time. They then set out to see the highland coos.

They enjoyed the ride over and if truth be told, there may have been a wee race as the two four-wheelers sped up the road. When they spotted the hairy bovines, they pulled over.

"Woohoo, it's the blokes of Rossmoooore! Where have ya been keepin' yourselves?" Lulabelle said as she approached the fence.

"Ha! Nice to see ya too!" Socorro said. "Look what we brought ya."

Lulabelle turned and looked into the wee pail. "Neeps! My fav!"

Socorro pulled back. "Neeps? We brought carrots, cabbage and turnips!"

"Well, as I see it, yous brought carrots, cabbage and neeps!"

"Neeps are my favorite, too!" Belgium cried out as he galloped up. He used his wee hooves to pounce at Rory, playfully. Rory hopped back, spilling the bucket. All the veggies dumped in a heap just over the fence. The coos pushed at each other, going after the veggies greedily.

"Mooove over!" Annika cried out, swinging her hind quarters into Lulabelle.

"Ah, say, donnae be so roooood! You need to mooove!"

Belgium being the wee one dove in between their legs, snagging a neep.

"Ach, yous are all so greedy! I didnae mean to start a war." Rory said, with a chuckle. But the coos paid him no mind until the last cabbage leaf was consumed.

A thunderous sound alerted them that several giant Clydesdale horses were galloping over. They were in the next pasture, with just a flimsy fence separating them from the coos. But it, too, was electrified.

"Well, look at these beauties," Socorro said. Five white-nosed mares poked their heads over the fence, waiting for a pat down.

The boys rubbed each one's head and ears. "Such calm animals. Guess they are well trained." Rory said.

One of them whinnied. "Aye, we are trained. Our owner is kind and treats us well."

"Good to know." Socorro answered. "Sorry, but the coos ate all the treats! I'll bring extra next time. But hey, do you have any new news, from the grapevine?"

"Aye, they have news alright," said Lulabelle. "But hold on, it's nae gud news!"

"So, what is it?" Socorro pressed.

"Wolves! I know it's not new news, but we saw them again, jist last night!" The creature shouted so loudly, the lads took a collective step back. "I've seen them with my own eyes!" he cried.

"That's the same thing Jeepers said..." Belgium stopped mid-sentence. He had both said the name of the "messenger" and tattled on himself for eavesdropping. He pressed himself as low to the ground as he could in hopes no one noticed.

"Jeepers?" asked Rory.

"The marten." Annika noted. "He's our secret messenger, or he was our secret." she said playfully looking down at Belgium and giving him a big wink.

"Big dark things with glowing eyes," interrupted another Clydesdale, getting back on the topic of wolves. "It was dark and at a distance. They dare nae get close to us, since we are bigger and more powerful than they! But we're warning yous, Better keep an eye out. For yourselves and for the sheep."

"Aye! They seem rather mystical. I mean, are they even real?" a coo asked.

"Yes, that's what we are trying to figure out!" Socorro said. "Do you get a really eerie feeling when you see them? Like your skin starts crawling and chills pop up on your arms. I mean not arms, legs? And not skin, ah, fur?" Socorro asked.

"Yep, tha' describes it perfectly!" she answered.

"Aye, Jist as I suspected, they're nae real!" Lulabelle chimed in. "Tall tales from the creature gossip line! First Jeepers and now yous!"

"Bu' ya donnae know for sure they arenae real! Wha' are they if nae real?" Annika questioned. "Cover your ears, Belgium and run along noo." The wee calf wiggled his ears and galloped off. All of the treats were already gone and he wasn't about to risk getting into trouble for listening in.

"Yous were nae very thoughtful speakin' aboot such thin's in front of my wee calf!" Annika scolded.

"True. I'm sorry about that. I'll be more thoughtful next time." Socorro said. He had forgotten how sensitive these furry beasties were. Besides he didn't want to terrify this wee calf.

"Yes, I do believe they are real! Just because they don't exist in the physical realm here on this island, doesn't mean they don't exist in the spiritual realm." He paused so they had time to think about it.

"Wolves mean trouble anyway you look at it." Annika mused.

"I remember some verses about wolves in sheep's clothes or something like that," Socorro added. "They're crafty and deceptive."

"But how do we fight wolves if they only exist in the spiritual realm?" Annika asked.

"The Bible tells us we are to use love, patience, and self-control as weapons and prayer as our direct cell phone to God. For humans anyway. Guess you ladies don't have cell phones!" Socorro said.

They all laughed.

"Socorro, we'd better get back. I want to get my pup today. Seems we've been here a long time, and it must be almost time for lunch." Rory said anxiously. "I cannae give your dad any doubts about me taking care of my pup."

Socorro glanced at his watch, "You're right, we need to hurry." He turned back toward the four-wheeler and then stopped. "I'm hopin' those wolves stay away and we all stay safe!"

The horses flicked their tails as they swatted at flies, then slowly sauntered away.

"Donnae stay away too long, pals!" Lulabelle called after the lads.

"We loved the neeps! Hope yous have more for next time!" Annika said, swishing her tale.

"Bye, thanks for the update." The boys waved, then they hopped on the four-wheelers.

"That's the second warning we received about the wolves. It really sounds like they may be part of the Calignocity, the evil beasts that Kristal and I encountered on the mountain." Socorro told Rory as they fastened on their helmets.

"And must be connected to all the mysterious red eyes we've seen around this island."

But as soon as the strap was secured, he sped off. Rory fell in behind, dodging his dust, as they raced back to the castle.

CHAPTER 21

THE ACCIDENT

After lunch, Rory hurried to Grammy and Pop's room. He knocked politely and waited. Finally, he was going to get his pup, Brandi Brindle. He heard scuffling inside and then a sudden, "Yeow!"

"Oh, no! Are you okay?" Grammy shouted.

Rory pushed the door open, concerned by the sounds he heard. He gasped when he saw Pop lying on the floor in front of the fireplace, his arm twisted behind him.

Pop moaned. "My arm, I think I broke it!"

Rory rushed over. "Jist lie still and I'll get help." He used his phone to call Socorro. Thankfully the call went through. The stone walls of the castle often interfered with reception.

"Hurry and get the doctor! Pop has fallen and is hurt!" Rory shouted as soon as Socorro answered. "Yes, I'm keeping him still. But hurry. He needs a doctor right away."

Socorro found his dad and quickly told him that Pop needed help. He then rushed up as fast as he could. "Pop!" he cried out when he saw him.

Pop cleared his throat. "Don't worry, boy, I just hurt my arm. I'm not dyin' or anything. See to your Grammy." He winked at Socorro despite his pain.

Since Rory was keeping Pop still, Socorro went over to Grammy and took her arm. He eased her onto the sofa and sat down beside her. He put his arm around her shoulders and reminded her to pray. Foster snuggled up against her feet, offering comfort. Rory took a quilt from the bed and covered Pop.

Soon the whole family gathered in the room, "Making too much fuss." Pop complained.

After a long wait, the doctor arrived. "Excuse me, let me by please" the doctor said.

"Let's clear out and let the doctor work," Kristal advised. Rory scooped up Brandi and they cleared the room except for Grammy who refused to leave Pop's side.

As they waited in the hall, they began to question Rory. "Please, tell us what happened!" they all cried at once.

"I'm not sure. I knocked on the door and then I heard a loud noise. Grammy called out and I rushed in and saw him lyin' on the floor. I guess he tripped or slid or something tryin' to answer the door. Makes me feel bad for disturbin' them!" He lowered his eyes and stared at the floor.

"It's not your fault, Rory. It sounds like an accident to me. Let's all go downstairs. We'll pray while we wait on news from the doctor." Kris said.

They formed a circle in the sitting room, grasping hands. They all began to pray. Even some of the staff joined in. Everyone loved Pop! But it wasn't long until the doctor exited the elevator. The bell alerted them to his arrival.

"Good news, everyone. I don't believe he broke anything. But he must wear a sling on his sore arm for a week or two. And don't worry, I have given him a pill for the pain. A few days of rest and he'll be as good as new." He approached Rory.

"You did everything just right by keeping him still and calm. I might need you for an assistant in the near future!" He laughed and patted the boy on the back. Rory felt a wee bit better. "But for now, I think the pets all need to be housed someplace else. Your granddad said he tripped over one of the wee pups. He hurt himself trying not to hurt the pup. But best not to take chances, now they are bigger and running about."

"Of course! We should have thought of that earlier! Would you like a pup, doctor?" Adara asked, smiling.

"Well, maybe. Let me ask my wife about that, and I will let you know." he answered.

"You know, I was thinkin' I need a pup at the lighthouse to keep me company." Gee spoke up. "I'll pick me out a wee pal today!"

"You pick one out and I'll keep it with me until it's a bit bigger," Hamish volunteered. "We donnae need a repeat of what happen'd with Pop!"

"And Rory and I will see if any of the villagers want one." Socorro said. He glanced at Rory for his approval. He nodded in agreement.

"In the meantime, Foster and her pups can stay in my room," Socorro volunteered. "And I'll keep Gee's pup with me during the week when you're gone, Hamish."

"Thank you, Socorro. That's a great plan." Dad said. Socorro took off to get the pets relocated to his room. Everyone else resumed the work of getting ready for the fall festival.

"I'll make a sign to post in the village, advertising that we have puppies available." Ailsa said. "Or better yet, I'll make lots of flyers to hand out. Let's go print them, Kristal." The girls left together, chatting about what needed to be printed on the flyers.

Once the pups were all comfy near the fire in Socorro's room, he and Rory left to go into the village to ask around. Maybe they could find 'furever' homes for the pups.

"We need to hurry if we want to get there while the shops are still open. I also need to get some things for Brandi." Rory said. "I know they have dog items at the bait shop, let's go there first."

Rory, Socorro and Brandi meandered along, until a storm cloud suddenly popped up, drenching them. They rushed on to their destination. They entered, as a bell chimed announcing their presence in the bait shop.

"Well, look wha's blown in!" the clerk laughed. "You's got caught ou' in the storm with no gear. Here, I have an ole' towel to wipe the pup." He reached under the counter, brought out the towel and then tossed it to the boys.

"Great! Ta." Rory said. "Yes, we rushed off withou' even grabbin' a brolly."

"What brings yous in?" he asked.

"I need some things for me new pet. Let's see, a leash, a harness and a bed. And I need food and treats." Rory spurted out.

"And a few toys," Socorro added. "If you don't keep some chewy toys close, she'll eat your shoes!"

They all laughed.

"Why, tha's quite a list. But, aye, I have most of those things. The section in the back right corner will be where ya need to look."

Just then, the bell jingled, as Ailsa and Kristal rushed in. But unlike the boys, they had an umbrella and jumpers which kept them dry.

"Fancy meeting you here." Kristal said.

"May we put a flyer in your window, Mr. McMurray?" Ailsa asked. "We need to find homes for five puppies right away! Pop fell over one of 'em today and hurt his arm!"

"Five? I thought there were six more!" Socorro said.

"Well, there were eight, then Rory and Gee each took one, and I believe the doctor is taking one, so that leaves five." Kristal said. Socorro shrugged.

Mr. McMurray agreed to them hanging a poster. He handed the girls a piece of tape and they secured it to the window. "Ta!" Ailsa called and the girls scurried out, looking for more places to post their message.

The boys took their time shopping for the things Rory needed for Brandi. In fact, they took so long, Mr. McMurray cleared his throat and reminded the boys he would be closing up the shop soon.

Rory ended up choosing a red harness and leash and put them on the wiggly pup. He just wanted her to get used to the feel of it, for now. He quickly gathered the rest of the items, which included a small rawhide chew and a toy mouse that squeaked.

Rory felt accomplished and proud. He'd paid for the items with the money he'd earned himself. And now he was a pet owner, something he'd always dreamed of!

Someone to love and someone to love me, he thought.

CHAPTER 22

REFLECTIONS

Kristal and Ailsa headed back to the castle and went to work moving furniture, setting things up and sorting. Even though they were nearing exhaustion, they still had a bit of time to kill before dinner, so they pushed on. Kristal was excited about an idea she had!

"Why not hang a large disco ball from the ceiling near the window?" she said.

"That's a great idea!" Ailsa responded.

They worked together and secured the ball on a hook that hung at just the right height. The South window got plenty of daylight and when the sun shone through the ball, light danced around the room in dozens of wee glittery dots!

Ailsa giggled! "Wha' a light show!" she yelped. She spun around in the center of the room chasing the dots like she'd seen her wee cat do!

"Enjoy it now, the sun will be going down soon." Kristal said as she stretched out on her mattress and watched the ball spin. Without thinking about it, she held her hand up and admired the way her ring looked on her finger. It had a sparkle of its own!

She said aloud musingly, "This reminds me of God's light reflecting off of us. He is the light source, like the sun. We are the reflectors, like the disco ball. When we follow Him, we reflect His light!"

"True," Ailsa said, but then she noticed her ring. "Kristal, are you engaged?" she gasped!

"No, not yet. But I'm promised to Hamish. I mean, we promised each other that we wouldn't date anyone else. To seal the promise, he gave me this ring! But back to the reflections, it reminded me of something. I want to share a story with you."

"Okay." Ailsa agreed. She sat down on the edge of the bed. She studied the wee ring on Kristal's finger. "It's brilliant..." she whispered.

Kristal smiled. "Thanks! But here's the story. Remember when I told you about Socorro and I being lost on a mountain? Well, there was a time when a flock of hummingbirds flew together to form colorful shapes for us. It was like looking into a giant kaleidoscope! The birds were all different colors, and the sun reflected off their feathers as they formed beautiful patterns. I wish you could've been there; it was like peeking into heaven and seeing a tiny bit of God's glory!"

"Wow!" Ailsa said. "Tha' gives me goose flesh!" she hugged Kristal impulsively. "Thanks for being my pal. I know I'm goin' to love sharin' a room with ya. It's brilliant!"

Ailsa went over to her bed, laid back and watched the dazzle of the disco orb. They had both worked hard, and the room was absolutely lovely! The rich colors of the purple and gold accessories were offset by the beige and neutrals of the wall colors, giving the room a cozy effect. *Kristal really has talent*, Ailsa mused! *And I get to enjoy it! And I'm excited for her. I'd love to get a ring like that someday! Maybe she'll ask me to be in her weddin'!*

~

As the boys passed the dock, they noticed the tramp steamer was there again. It was a terrible reminder for Rory, forcing him to remember the blokes aboard and the job he'd left. He shivered and pulled his hat down farther on his forehead.

The weary deckhands moved about the deck like lizards, slinking and darting, trying to stay out of the line of fire from their wicked boss. Even though he had changed his appearance, Rory grew nervous that someone might recognize him. But his pup was growing restless, and in the worst timing ever, wiggled out of his arms!

He grabbed for her leash, but she was fast, and he couldn't catch her. Now she was racing toward the steamer!!

"Stop, Brandi," he croaked out. He chased after her, his heart racing. Socorro joined him in the chase, when suddenly they found themselves nose to nose with two of the deckhands.

"Whoa, blokes! Yous cannae get on the boat!" one of the men said.

"We're not getting on the boat! We're trying to catch our dog!" Socorro yelled, pointing to the pup that had cowered on the boardwalk, just a few feet away. Another bloke reached down and grabbed the pup by the harness strap. He grinned at them with yellow, broken, teeth as he clutched the wee creature in his grimy hands. He swung her out over the water.

"Hey, I wonder if it can swim! What do ya think fellas, should I drop it in?" he laughed wickedly.

"Stop!" Rory yelled. He plunged at the bloke, grabbing for the frightened pup. But the other two deckhands grabbed Rory. He squirmed and fought, but it was no use. One of them twisted his arm behind his back and Rory cried out in pain. Socorro tried to come to his aid but was hit squarely in the jaw by a fist, knocking him to the ground. They were then drug aboard, the pup still in the hands of the grubby sailor. Socorro looked up and saw a large bird of prey flying overhead. He whistled loudly and the bird turned in their direction. It was the peregrine falcon, a prominent pal of theirs named Perry.

"Get help!!" Socorro yelped. "Hurry, we're in trouble!"

The sailors laughed, "Who you yelling at? There's no one aboot! I'm afraid your luck has run out!" They shoved the boys toward a set of steep steps that led below deck.

"Tie 'em up! Guess we got two new hands noo." the bloke laughed. "And drown the dog or choke it. I donnae care which, jist get rid of it!"

Rory gulped! But he didn't make a noise because he recognized the man speaking, it was the captain! He ducked his head, hoping he wouldn't be recognized; because if he did, he'd walk the plank for sure, just like in his dream!

"Run Brandi, Run!" Socorro called as the pup wriggled out of the bloke's arms, hit the deck and ran down the loading plank, trailing the lead behind.

"Let it go, we are aboot to shove off." The captain shouted, waving off the hands.

Rory and Socorro both breathed a sigh of relief knowing the puppy got away! He prayed that someone on the island would find her and look after her.

But they weren't as fortunate. They were taken below and tied to thick wooden uprights in the dark hull. When the trap door slammed shut, they frantically struggled against the ropes that bound them, but to no avail. The rope was too thick. And with every move, the course bindings dug into their wrists, cutting their skin. They were in total darkness, and in the quietness below, they heard the repetitious drip of water somewhere.

Rory sighed. "I was jist gettin' used to living the high life! Noo I'm back where I started. But not only me, I've got you into this mess, too. Will you forgive me, Socorro?" he said sadly. "At least my pup got away, maybe she'll be alright!"

"Hey, we are just at the beginning of this adventure!" Socorro said. "I've learned that man, wolves, elements or whatever can be after us, but if God is for us, no one can be against us! Remember the lesson from Romans 8:31 Dad taught us? Besides, I called out to Perry, a falcon who has become a pal, and he flew away to get help. And if the family finds Brandi all alone, they'll know to come look for us. Just wait and see."

The loud roar of the engine let them know the tramp steamer was leaving the dock. But instead of fear and panic, Socorro chose to trust in the Lord. He'd been in dark scary places before, and God had come through for him. He knew if he just waited, help would come. Rory, however, looked like he was sweating bullets, so Socorro decided to tell him about his experiences.

"Hey, Rory, now is a good time to tell you what I went through a couple of years ago. It's a very long story, but we have nothing but time right now. When I was trapped in a net and lying on a mountain about to freeze to death, a wise creature taught me this poem. I know it is simple and childlike, but I think it is appropriate for us right now." He closed his eyes and saw himself alone and afraid on the mountain. He envisioned his little bunny friend and felt again the emotions of that day. He swallowed. "Here's how it goes:"

> I will not doubt, and I will not fear,
> 'cuz God my Father sent his angels
> here. When the beasts arrive, and I'm
> filled with fear, I will always remember
> that God's angels are near!

"I was facing many dark creatures of the mountain that day, much like the danger we are facing right now. But I found out that God was with me. He was with me then and He is still with us now. That's one of his promises, that he will never leave us."

"Yes, but its plenty hard to nae be afraid when you're tied up in the bottom of a boat with a bunch of pirates above!" Rory said.

It was then they saw them! All around them in the dark, the red flashing eyes stood out like beacons on a runway! The room was full of them, every corner, above, beside and below them!

"It's the beasts!" Socorro called out. "They are trying to make us fear and doubt! I know you're near, Angels. Help us be brave!"

Everything grew still but the pounding of their hearts in their ears. A cool breeze drifted through the room and Socorro began to chant: "God's angels are near, angels are near, I will not doubt, and I will not fear." He sang it over and over and soon Rory joined in. They sang louder and louder, and then just as suddenly as they came, all of the eyes vanished.

Then a light, so bright it nearly blinded them, appeared from above! The hatch was thrown back, and a rough voice yelled: "Oi! Cut the noise. Do ya think you're a bunch of songbirds? Maybe those ropes aren't tight enough, eh?"

"Sorry! We'll keep the noise down." Socorro called out. "Any chance we could get out of here? I bet you could use the help of a couple of strong lads up there?"

"Yous jist want to escape! Wait until we're out at sea. There will be plenty of work for you then." he laughed wickedly. *Slam!!* The trap door banged shut jarring them and once again they were in total darkness.

CHAPTER 23

BAD NEWS

TAP TAP TAP Pause. TAP TAP.

"Wha's tha'?" Ailsa sat up quickly on her bed and turned to find the source of the sound. A puffin was pecking on the window with its beak!

"It's Deemer! Aye, wha's wrong?" Ailsa crooned. "Quick, open the window!" Kristal hurried over and lifted the sash. Deemer had never come this far from the cliffs and had never shown up at the castle, before.

"Something is amiss!" she grunted out her message to Ailsa rapidly.

"What is going on?" Kristal cried out.

"Deemer says she was told by Perry, the falcon, that the lads have been captured! They're on a boat and are headed out to sea! Socorro told Perry to get help. We must hurry before the boat is too far away!"

"Which lads? Socorro, Hamish, Rory?"

Ailsa turned back to Deemer, and again Deemer grunted out her message. "She says Socorro for sure and they donnae know who else. Two young blokes for certain!"

Kristal was already using her cell. "Hamish! Are you okay? Good, we need your help right away. Socorro and Rory have been forced onto a boat, and they are going, I mean gone...Yeah, I'll try to calm down, but we must hurry. They've been kidnapped...Yes, we're at the castle...Okay, see you in a minute."

Meanwhile, Ailsa thanked her friend Deemer for letting them know what was happening. Then she hurried from the room and down to the main level. Kristal was just a few steps behind.

"Mum, Adara! The lads are in trouble!!" Ailsa shouted. She hurriedly told them what she had just learned. But everything seemed to be playing out in slow motion! She felt so dizzy and quickly sat down and put her head between her knees! *Slow breaths, Ailsa. There is no time for this*, she told herself. *We must hurry if we ever want to see those lads again!*

The adults scurried about, grabbing jackets and shouting instructions chaotically. Hamish and Gee burst through the door. Kris left his office to see what all the shouting was about. Everyone was talking at once until Kris whistled!

"Wait, slow down. We need a plan! Adara, call the maritime police. Mary, gather flashlights and any other supplies you think we'll need. Hamish, Gee and I will go after them. The rest of you need to stay here and pray." They all moaned in protest.

"No, I mean it now. You must stay here with your phones on and fight this battle on your knees. We will need the prayer support. Now, those going with me, let's go!"

"Wait, why don't I go to the lighthouse and watch for the boat through my telescope and tell the authorities if I see them?" Gee spoke up.

"Excellent idea! Let's split up then." Kris said.

After a bit more discussion, Ailsa was allowed to go along since she could communicate with the birds. But poor Pop was almost beside himself. "If I hadn't hurt my shoulder, I would be going with them!" he lamented.

"Well, you're needed here more than ever. Mom and Grammy are upset; we're all upset. We need you to lead us in prayer. Let's gather around the fire and pray!" Kristal said.

She hated being left behind, too, since so many of those she cared about were in jeopardy right now! She looked out the window; it was so dark! She lifted her chin in determination. Now is the time to pray! It was as vital to their success as those actually looking for the boys!

The staff and family that were still at home circled their chairs close to the fire and joined hands. They called out the names of each person to God: "Socorro...Rory...Kris...Hamish...Ailsa...Gee! Please give them wisdom and keep them safe. And Father, help them to defeat the enemy and get back home! Amen."

CHAPTER 24

THE FOX AND THE PUP

Gee entered the lighthouse and made his way up the staircase much more quickly than he usually did. The young lads were in danger, and he wanted to do all he could to help. The Frazier family had done so much to help him and Hamish in the past few years. If it wasn't for them, he would not be living here in this lighthouse and fulfilling his dream!

On the observation deck, he focused the telescope on the sea. It was rough tonight; the waves were rapid and thick. He turned his telescope to scan in the direction of the dock. There it was! The tramp steamer was lit up like the city of London, making it easy to spot. He radioed to the maritime police and gave them the approximate coordinates, then steadied his gaze, determined to follow the boat until it was out of sight.

Kris barreled down the rough road only slowing for the largest potholes. His truck's headlights appeared dim in the deep darkness that had fallen.

"Watch out!" Hamish yelled. Just ahead a wee animal was square in the middle of the road! They skidded to a stop. With a gasp, Ailsa jumped from the truck and scooped up the wee pup. It was Brandi! She dodged the sloppy kisses the pup tried to give her. It was terribly frigid and she shivered as she clung to the wet, mud-covered pup.

Nearby, a sudden movement in the grass caught Ailsa's eye. A beautiful red fox peered at her, his shiny fur glistening in the car lights. The fox nodded its head, then turned and disappeared into the tall grass. Brandi had an escort! Maybe the fox was part of the Scintilliant that Socorro talked about. He told her how the good creatures on *Mystic Mountain* were angelic beings that helped him and his family. *Were they here on this Island too?* She would ask him what he thought about that later. Suddenly, the thought of him not being there later, overcame her and she started to cry. She stood there paralyzed in the cold, the pup in her arms and tears pouring down her cheeks.

Kris sounded the truck horn. She jumped, then hurried back over. She handed the pup to Hamish. He wrapped her in a blanket they had brought along, drying her off as best as he could. As soon as Ailsa closed her door, they sped ahead stopping at the dock. Ailsa continued to sob, she just couldn't stop. Hamish took her hand. The warmth of it was reassuring and she was able to get a grip.

There were only a few lights in the area, dimly illuminating the board-walk where the ships landed. This was a wee island and rarely would you find ships docked at the end of the pier, especially at night.

And as usual, it was deserted tonight. Whatever boat was there earlier in the day, was gone now! But Deemer and Perry circled the area. Ailsa spotted them. "I need to see wha's up," she cried as she got out of the truck. Hamish was up to his neck in wet puppy, so Kris got out with her. They hurried up the board walk. When they stopped near the sea, the birds landed close by.

"They have a plan!" Ailsa exclaimed. "They told us not to worry. They have beastie pals everywhere on standby and if anyone can find the lads, it's them!" She was seriously shaking now, the rain biting at her skin. Kris put his arm around her and directed her toward the truck.

"We must get you back where its dry. The birds are so much better equipped to move about out here. We need to trust God and let Him work!" The crew headed back. Finding the pup somehow gave them hope they would find the others.

~

The rough sea was taking a toll on the two lads tied in the hold of the steamer. Socorro felt dizzy and his wrists were chaffed from the rough rope. His cheek felt swollen and sore. Rory fought nausea that plagued him in the dark shifting quarters. They needed fresh air!

Just when they were at the height of misery, the hatch door overhead opened. A deckhand growled orders at them to get on the deck.

"We could if we weren't tied to poles." Socorro shouted back.

The scrawny, smelly deckhand pulled a large knife. The boys sucked in their breaths collectively. He wobbled down the ladder, turned and grinned. "So, yous want me to cut ya loose! I hope my hands are steady, been shaking a bit lately. Now who's first?" He approached Rory and with a swift move cut the rope! Rory grabbed his wrist and jumped back. "Wha's wrong, lad? You scared?" He seemed to find that hilarious and doubled over laughing. Another sailor happened by and yelled, "Wha's so funny down there? Hurry up and quit shirkin' your work!"

The deckhand growled and cut Socorro's ropes. "Yous better nae give me any grief or your DEAD!" Socorro stood up. He towered over the scrawny guy. The deckhand took a step back. "Wow, yous a big'un. Well, you know wha' they say, the bigger they are, the harder they fall!" Again, he laughed at his own joke. No one else seemed to find any amusement in it. Socorro gave him a stern look and stepped around him. He hurriedly climbed the ladder to the deck. *Fresh air!* He took in a few big gulps. Rory followed him to the railing where they could look out at the roiling seas.

"Get over here so's I can show yous wha's to be done," the scrawny guy yelled. They reluctantly followed him to the stern where another hatched door and ladder led below to a galley. Piles and piles of dishes sat in half barrels around the room. "Kitchen duty, get busy!" the guy yelled.

The boys looked at one another. "Hey, we can handle this!" Socorro turned on the tap where steaming hot water ran into a stainless-steel sink. He poured in the detergent and let it fill up. "I wonder when our help will get here?" he whispered close to Rory's ear. Rory just shrugged. He was busy adding the dishes to the sink. If they didn't appear busy, they would be punished, for sure.

"I'm jist thinkin' aboot Brandi. I had her for such a short time and noo she's gone. You heard wha' the beasties were sayin' aboot wolves. Poor pup!" He set the pot down a bit too hard. "These slugs make me so mad! If me dog gets hurt, they will pay!"

Socorro felt for Rory. He knew how it was to worry about a pet. He had chased Foster many times trying to keep her out of trouble. But there was nothing they could do now but concentrate on the job at hand and pray. They were in a good deal of danger themselves.

A loud clap of thunder sounded and the boat shook. They heard shouts outside. The ship was now seriously rocking! What was happening? Socorro pushed Rory and whispered loudly, "Hide!"

The boys rushed through the galley and around large pipes to the engine area. They squeezed into a mop closet and held their breaths. They armed themselves with mops and buckets, ready to fight if anyone entered. But apparently no one was even looking for them. The storm was wreaking havoc, and the crew was busy locking things down.

"There's the coppers!" someone shouted.

"Full speed ahead, we can outrun them!" the captain ordered. But the waves grew with each passing moment, and the ship was being tossed about. One powerful wave washed over the deck threatening the crew. "Get below! We'll be washed overboard!" another shouted.

Through the view finder of his scope, the police captain became concerned. They had the tramp steamer in their sights, but the sea was growing rougher by the minute! The massive waves threatened to capsize their tiny boat. An alarm sounded. They were getting gale warnings on the radio as the storm strengthened. Rain was coming down in torrents. If this kept up, they'd have to turn back.

Gee radioed Kris. "Looks like the police are chasing the steamer. But gale warnings are going out. Wait! Looks like they are turning back!"

"Who? The police? No, they can't give up! Those pirates will get away with our boys onboard!" Kris pounded his fist on the steering wheel.

"Please help them, Lord." Ailsa prayed, her chin quivering. But with torrential rain coming down, there was nothing they could do but return to the castle, before the sketchy road became impassable.

CHAPTER 25

THE LONG NIGHT

The boys crept out of the closet. It was dark, but they had the light from the engines instrument panels to help them get around. *Now what?* No one seemed to be looking for them. Maybe they had forgotten about them altogether? They found a corner in the back and sat down to think. "I'm starvin'!" Rory said. "And I know where they keep the supplies. Let's go see if we can find somethin' ta eat."

Socorro followed Rory, crouched over, hiding behind the equipment as they made their way toward the supply cupboard. *Why was it so quiet?* Something weird was happening. Or, maybe, the thunder was so loud they couldn't hear anything else. The ship rocked so badly that the boys could barely stand. They hung on to whatever they could. Suddenly they heard a loud creak!

"That was alarming! Are we going to make it? Hurry, I'm thinking this ship is going to bust up in the sea! We need to get out of here and see what is going on!" Socorro shouted. They had just made it to the food closet so they grabbed all the packaged snacks they could hold as well as several bottles of water.

"Look, there's a knapsack. Stuff as much food and water in there as you can." Rory directed.

The boys held on as the boat veered to the side. They fell against the wall, disoriented.

"Get to the deck! We must get out of this hull before the ship is upside down!" Rory shouted.

Suddenly, lights came on and a loud alarm sounded. The captain was on the speaker, "Abandon ship! Mayday, mayday!"

Since the boys had not been provided with life jackets, Rory made a beeline to the storage container that held the equipment. He pulled two of them out and passed one to Socorro. They donned them as fast as they could. Now to get to a lifeboat. They heard a loud creak, and then a loud groan! The boat began to sink!

It was too late to look for lifeboats. The boys scrambled and climbed until they could pull themselves up on the railing. There they saw that two lifeboats had already launched! Several crew members were in them, bouncing around on the rough sea.

"Jump!" Rory yelled. The boys jumped out as far from the ship as possible! They were both strong swimmers and soon they were able to reach one of the boats. The sailors aboard stared at them, not offering to pull them aboard.

"We have food and water!" Rory shouted, "Please help us on!"

Someone tossed a life buoy their way and they were able to hang on to it until they could board the wee vessel. When they were settled in the boat, the boys looked into the wide, frightened eyes of those aboard. They were surprised to see that they were no older than they were! These lads had escaped the hard hand-to-mouth life of Liverpool streets, only to scrape by again as the crew of the "The Sea Witch" tramp steamer.

There were seven aboard, counting Socorro and Rory.

One of the blokes tossed a rope toward Rory. "Tie yourselves in!" he shouted.

The two shrugged into the seat harnesses, then tied the rope around their waists. They shivered violently. Hypothermia was a given unless they dried off!

Rory remembered something he had learned while a sailor on the ship. They needed to wring out their clothes and get the thermal tarps spread over them. He shouted out instructions. Miraculously, the blokes followed them as they found the tarps on the lifeboat and soon had two of them unfurled and secured over their heads. They took turns wringing out their wet clothing and balancing themselves in the boat. Once most of the moisture was out of their clothes, their own body heat would help them get warm. If they survived the violent waves, that is. They hunkered down. Socorro was praying but he heard several of the teens whimpering in the dark.

Socorro prayed out loud, hoping to comfort the others. "Heavenly Father, we need your help to survive! I know You see us and You know where we are, so please save us here in the sea. Please, if it be Your will, save us."

One of the boys cried. "Please save me, not jist from the sea, but from me sins! I've done bad things jist to survive and 'ave forgotten about you, God!"

Another boy echoed the prayer. All of them knew that their fate was in the hands of God the Father, and if He decided to let them perish, they would need to be right in their hearts.

Rory spoke up, "God, you healed me from deep pain and scars, jist a few days ago. Please save us from the depths of this icy sea! Save us from our fears, as well!"

All of the blokes cried and prayed, tossing on the giant waves through the night. Promises were made to God, that if he saved them, they would serve Him. It was the plea of the desperate!

Sometimes they sang the song that held so much comfort for Rory, Amazing Grace. Sometimes they were silent. The night was torturously long. Once the waves calmed a tad, and they were a bit warmer under the tarp, they were finally able to fall into an exhausted sleep.

Four enormous angels diligently held up the corners of the life raft. God had heard the prayers of the lads in distress. He didn't take them out of the storm, but He was there with them through it all.

CHAPTER 26

DESPERATE PRAYERS

Out in the lighthouse, Gee was sending up more prayers. There was no letup in the storm. The lightning flashed and the thunder boomed, as Gee focused his telescope toward where he'd last seen the boat. But there was nothing but utter darkness. He feared the worst; that the ship had sunk. What other explanation was there for the lights to disappear from the inky water?

He lowered the scope and sat down, weary and tense. He assumed the stance of prayer with bowed head and hands clasped tightly and begged God to save his friend, Socorro and the lad, Rory, from the depths of the sea. They needed a miracle. *Please, Father, save the laddies! I know You are powerful and hold all of us in the palm of Your hand. Please save them!* He sighed, and finished with, *Nevertheless, may Your will be done. Amen.*

Back at the castle the family, too, was earnestly praying, quietly, yet fretfully. Hamish and Kristal sat next to each other, their hands clasped. She was crying softly. This was an all too familiar feeling for her. Socorro was in grave danger, and she was left behind to pray. How many times had she found herself in this place on *Mystic Mountain*? Too many times, to count! *This should be a fun, exciting time, the entire family getting ready for the upcoming festival. But it all changed in a blink! That's how it is in life;* she thought, *you're innocently enjoying special moments, then surprise! Its mind blowing at how fast things can change!*

The others sat in various places around the room staring at the fire, dazed and overwhelmed. A haunting thought was on their minds. *How could the boys possibly survive in this monstrous storm?*

Kris was beside himself. Inactivity was the last thing he wanted right now! He needed to be out there searching! He paced around the massive parlor, nervous energy plunging through his veins. He felt so out of control. He closed his eyes and remembered a moment on *Mystic Mountain* when he had felt the same way. Lost kids, no direction, no hope.

Then he remembered a lesson he learned. *There was always hope! The boys were in God's hands, and He loved them even more than he and Adara did.* He chided himself. *You'd think I'd have figured this out after all I've been through!* But he was beginning to realize that faith isn't built during one big lesson, but by moments in life, one block at a time.

A consistent negative question kept plaguing him. *Just because God helped us before, doesn't mean He will continue, does it?* He shook his head. He must fight against these thoughts and the paralyzing fear they brought with them. The only solution was prayer and scripture.

Unfortunately, he was too restless to sit and meditate. He needed to move! *That's why praying is the last thing I want to do right now!* But even if he didn't feel like doing it, he knew it was what he needed the most. So, he sat down, opened his Bible and rustled through the pages to the index and looked up the word 'fear'. Isaiah 41:12-13 was listed. He read it slowly.

"Though you search for your enemies, you will not find them. Those who wage war against you will be as nothing at all. For I am the Lord your God who takes hold of your right hand and says to you, Do not fear; I will help you."

He stopped and read it out loud to the family and friends gathered there. "I want you to know that I am full of fear right now, same as you. But even though we don't know the future, we know the One who holds our right hand. And His promise is that He will help us. We must focus on the 'Do not fear' part. If I could see into that boat right now, I bet Socorro and Rory are surrounded by angels. And" —he slowed for emphasis— "I bet they are influencing their captors to do the right thing!" He looked around the room.

"Since we are forced to sit here and wait this out, let's keep praying. We must keep praying and never give up! Let's pray out loud. Who wants to start?"

And that is exactly what they did! As the storm raged outside, the war raged inside! They prayed fervently, believing God would answer. They prayed and prayed.

But sometime in the deep night, Ailsa and wee Brandi fell asleep. They were too tired to stay awake any longer. They slept soundly, curled up on a sofa next to Mary. Kris' words had taken root. Ailsa knew that God always keeps His promises!

CHAPTER 27

DELIVERED

Socorro awoke to a coughing fit. He felt stiff and sore. Others on the tiny vessel started stirring around him, murmuring and coughing as well. The warmth of the sun let him know it was fully engaged in the sky. In fact, it was hot and stifling! They threw back the thermal blanket and blinked in the sudden blaze of light. They were still in the midst of the sea, but it was as calm as bathwater. "We made it!" Socorro cried out, in a scratchy voice.

They scanned the sea for any sign of life. Nothing. Not even a sign of the other lifeboat or the tramp steamer. Sea birds squawked overhead. That had to be a good sign! *No birds, no land, sea birds, island!*

"I know some of the sea creatures near our island. We have become friends over the years, and they will help us. If you see a whale or dolphin, holler! I'll see if they will tow us in."

"Wha'?", one of the boys questioned. "Are you sayin' you talk to the animals? You tha' guy Dolittle or somethin'?" he laughed.

"Yeah, it sounds weird, but I've seen it with me own eyes. He gets the beasties to listen to 'im. Wha' other ideas do yous have?" Rory asked, his face turning red.

They all shook their heads. "We need food and water, I know tha'," a young lad said. "Water, for sure."

They looked around the boat. There were several insulated chest containers. One of the boys opened one and found it full of tin cans. "Look! Food like they have for the military. Open those other containers and maybe we'll find water!"

They searched each chest. They found canteens of water, first aid supplies, and fishing equipment. For blokes who are used to surviving the streets, they were set! And Rory still had the knapsack that was stuffed with food, although it was soggy and crumpled. At least the snacks were sealed.

They ate a bit of the food and drank some water. They knew they must conserve some, like a ration. But it was hard. They were all parched.

Introductions were made as they ate. Rory was surprised he hadn't seen these blokes before. They weren't on the boat when he was hired on. Must be newbies. But by the sounds of their accents, they were from the same area as Rory.

"I'm Tad, this 'ere's Thomas, tha's Boyd, Jori and Hayden." Tad pointed at each one as he introduced them. "We're all from the streets of Liverpool. The Cap'n forced us aboard that boat and made us work for him. He gave us food, but other than threats and blows, nothin' else! It was kidnappin'!" The others grunted and nodded in agreement. "But who cares anyway? Nobody's lookin' for us, and we might as well have been on that boat as the street! Ey, pals?" Tad said.

"Right. No one cares aboot us." Boyd agreed. The lads all agreed, mumbling their reply.

"No one but God! Donnae forge' how He helped us survive last night! And we need 'im noo more'n eva!

I know firsthand how God can save. He helped me many times. I know it's a bit weird talkin' aboot God and all, but we must keep prayin'." Rory stressed.

The boys all looked a bit confused. Yeah, they had prayed in the stress of the storm. But was God really there for a bunch of teenaged orphans?

"Besides, I told a friend of mine to go for help as we were being taken on the boat. I'm sure someone is looking for us now! If Perry, our falcon friend, couldn't get help, I'm sure some of the sea creatures will." Socorro knew he risked sounding "weird", but if telling them the truth made him weird, he was okay with that.

He and Rory talking about God, was sure to offend some, but that's just how it works. Other believers had helped him deal with rejection in the past. They reminded him that the Bible says Jesus was rejected, too, and even killed!

"Tell me yous stories, how ya were taken aboard the *Sea Witch*." Rory said, changing the subject.

"Me? Well, I was on the Liverpool streets 'cause I was kict ou' of the care home, too old. But there werenae no work. A gang took me in 'n taugh' me how to nic enough food to survive. Me job wa' to nic pastries. I snatched 'em and ran and sometimes I got 'em from the garbage bin at the end of the day. Some vendors wud wrap food in clean paper 'n lay it on top for us!

But one day, I got ta' the alley late and it was already dark. A bloke grabbed me from behin' and drug me off! I yelled and kicked, but he knoced me ou'! When I woke up, I was on the *Sea Witch*, moanin' with a 'orrible 'eadache!" Tad said.

"Yeah, well I was nae an orphan, but I run off after me da' beat me, again. I 'ad enough! I took off and at first, I was better off on me own. But I barely 'it the streets before the same bloke dru' me to the boat." Jori told them.

The stories were much the same throughout the wee group. They were all on the streets, either in a gang or surviving hand to mouth. Then they were drug to work as slaves on the pirate ship.

"Well, we will survive this! My family will help ya once we get back. We own a castle on *Mystic Island*, and we have plenty of rooms." Socorro said.

The boys all laughed. "Yeah, I bet!! That's why they foun' yous on the street and threw you on board. You're a big liar, bu' your stories are brillian'!" Boyd said, chuckling.

"Oi! Jist wai'! You'll see he's tellin' the truth!" Rory yelled. "Take me for instance. I wa' on the *Sea Witch*, but I jumped ship and landed on the island. His family took me in, gave me food and board. And even more, I learned aboot God and how He takes in all orphans!"

"Wha'ever. Me thinks yous got too much sea water in ya!" The blokes laughed again.

Socorro just shrugged. It did sound pretty far-fetched! Sometimes, even now, he wondered if his life was just a dream.

"Look, dolphins!" Thomas pointed out. Socorro jumped up, rocking the wee boat, water sloshing in over the sides. He leaned over and splashed the water with his palm, then whistled. The dolphins came and surrounded the vessel.

"Hey, pals!" Socorro cried out. "We're stuck in this boat! If I toss a rope, can you pull us to shore?"

The dolphins hung close by and even appeared to be nodding their heads. One raised up on his tail, his body almost totally out of the water and waited. The blokes were in awe!

"Rory, toss me the rope!" Socorro yelled.

"Yes, bu' donnae jerk aboot! This wee boat is too wobbly. You're goin' to throw us all ou'!" he replied as he tossed over the rope that was attached to the front of the lifeboat.

Socorro swung the rope like a lasso, and it fell into the sea. The rope barely hit the water before a dolphin snagged the loop and tossed it over its snout. The wee vessel jerked forward, flying across the surface of the water like the seabirds do!

The dolphins jumped and pulled, and the lads hung on for dear life! They laughed as they rapidly rode through the wake.

"It's like a circus ride!" Tad called out.

The group sat back and enjoyed the trip through the mystic waters. The dolphins took them as far as they could. When the water got too shallow, the lads hopped out and pulled the boat up onto the beach. Winded and tired, they collapsed on the cold sand. With the help of the sea creatures, they had landed!

CHAPTER 28

BRICKS AND BOTTLES

Mary lifted her weary body out of the chair. The fire was almost out and needed to be tended, but no one seemed to have enough energy to do the task. They were exhausted from the long vigil of the night and the worry and stress it held. So, she added another log to the fire then got busy in the kitchen putting on water for tea and coffee. *The family would be needin' breakfast.* She knew her tasks well and went through the motions of preparing the food automatically with little thought or effort.

Ailsa yawned and scooted the puppy and cat off her lap. They must have crawled up sometime in the night. Then it hit her, Socorro and Rory were still in danger! Ugh, she hated to wake up to such a reality, but here she was. She padded over to the kitchen in her bare feet and pushed the door open. What she saw made her gasp! Her mum was kneading bread, but she didn't look like her mum. Before her stood a tall bottle in her mum's dress and apron!

The bottle was crystal clear revealing red liquid inside. It was so full the liquid sloshed out the top of her and spilled onto the floor. There were scarlet puddles everywhere her mum had walked. Ailsa slowly entered the kitchen and sat down at the table, her mouth agape. *Was this the same sort of vision I had when I saw Rory wounded and bleeding? It must be! What does it mean*? She rubbed her eyes and put her head down on the table. *Lord, help me know what this means!*

She thought about it. Her mum was a vessel, a full vessel. But she was full of the wrong things. Ailsa could feel her fear, her doubts and the anxiety of not fully trusting in God. *She needs to empty herself of the old ways, the habit of worry,* Ailsa realized.

"Mum, can you come sit with me a wee minute?" Ailsa asked.

"I'm very busy right noo, pet. After breakfast I will." The bottle answered.

"No, mum, this cannae wait." Ailsa held a steady gaze at the tall bottle, still dripping liquid. "Please, you must." The bottle dried its hands on the apron, then wobbled over to the table, the liquid sloshing and spilling all the way. Ailsa shivered. It was so weird.

The bottle bent and sat, and Ailsa felt the cold liquid as it doused her. *Ugh, oppressive fear! Worry so heavy she could hardly sit up*. She was so full that she was spilling out on everyone else! It was all there.

"Mum, you're nae goin' to believe this, but I can see how you're feelin'. So scared and anxious! I know it's because the lads are in such danger, bu' ya must empty yourself of this! You're full and spillin' over! Let God fill ya with comfort and peace! But first ya must rid yourself of this other stuff."

Mary knew Ailsa was right. She *was* full of fear and doubt. She began to cry. And as she cried, she felt herself release all the negative feelings. She prayed and asked God to empty her.

Slowly the vessel began to morph. Soon Ailsa saw her mum sitting there, wiping her eyes with a corner of the apron.

"Ailsa, it's so hard to trust God in times like this! I donnae wan' ta make thin's worse for Adara and Kris by sharin' my own fears and wha' I think happened in the nigh'! We needed a miracle and I couldnae believe enough for one. Instead, I le' fear, anxiety and darkness fill me. But if God is speakin' to ya and showin' ya my feelin's, wee lass, then He's at work, noo isnae He!"

Mary straightened her back. She felt relief as peace washed over her. God was comforting her heart that had once been twisted with pain. Suddenly, she felt much lighter! She felt her heart soar upwards like a balloon when someone drops the string! It was then that she felt brave enough to believe that the lads would return home!

Adara was not faring much better. Kris was trying to comfort her, but she stood stiffly, her face stony and white.

Ailsa shook her head. Not Adara, too! Instead of seeing Socorro's mom standing by the fireplace, she saw a wall of bricks about her same height. All that was visible of the woman was the top of her head, her strawberry blonde hair sticking out!

Through all this, Adara, being the mom of one of the boys, was sick to her stomach. It felt like she had swallowed a bag of stones. Not only were the boys captured and held against their will, but the storm had raged, and the vessels on the sea were no match for something this strong. So, she had put up protective walls to keep out the pain.

"Adara!" Ailsa squealed. The wall jumped. "You're like a house of bricks! You've built 'em up so high, I can barely see ya! All's I see is your hair!" Ailsa covered her mouth with her hands in alarm.

At that moment, the walls began to crumble and Adara found herself in a heap on the floor.

Listen, child. I see your pain. I want to give you beauty for ashes. I know you've lost so much. Let me comfort you in the way only I can. Remember the lessons of the Mountain. Practice your faith!

The Holy spirit spoke to Adara's heart.

She hadn't realized that she had built such walls; walls that God couldn't penetrate unless she allowed Him in. She'd closed the door to her heart! But God was patiently seeking her. She blocked him with fear. *What if God says no to my prayer?* She couldn't take another loss. She'd been building these walls slowly through the years. With each loss, she'd become more walled off and now her precious son was in grave danger, again.

She closed her eyes and she was back on *Mystic Mountain*. Her fear and doubt were so strong, they were devouring her. A few bricks started to form a new wall that went up to her knees. That's okay, she thought, she needed her walls. She wrapped her arms around herself, as several more bricks stacked themselves up to her waist!

How can I come in, if you're so walled off? The small voice said. Then she realized how her lack of faith kept her from the one she needed most. She gulped.

She remembered the creature, Vesperinikin, the creature of God with black, flowing hair. "Practice your faith," she'd called out to her on the mountain. "Practice your faith!"

Adara squeezed her eyes shut. She shivered and cried, but finally, she felt the bricks crumbling! *Please release me, she prayed.* Now she could see God clearly, not just through the cracks of her wall. She was finally able let Him in. Fully in!

Now, my child, I can finally abide with you. This growth comes only through adversity. But I am able to give you peace in the storm. Embrace it. The Holy spirit prompted.

Kris came over and took her in his arms. He held her tight as he saw the sun rising through the window over her shoulder. The storm was finally over!

Ailsa turned and ran out the door. She needed a breath of fresh air! Besides, she needed to check on her wee sheep. But there on the wide front stoop sat Deemer!

"Deemer, I'm so glad to see ya!" Ailsa put her hand on the bird's head.

The bird nodded. "I'm glad to see ya, as well! But listen, I have grand news for ya! I was told by the falcon tha' the Clydesdales told him, tha' the marten told them, tha' the fox told him, tha' the sea turtle told him, tha' the porpoises told them, who were told by the dolphins tha' Socorro and Rory are alive!!" she was out of breath, now, but recovered enough to continue. "And there are a number of other lads with them that have survived as well." Deemer let out her breath and nearly collapsed after the statement! Ailsa jumped into the air, twirled and squealed!

"Where are they, then? Can ya take us to them? We need to find them and noo!"

"Hold on, hold on. Tha's the hard part. I have to follow all these beasties back to the dolphins and see if I can find them." Deemer told her.

Ailsa ran inside and spread the word. Soon the others were loading up in the vehicles. They would find the lads!

Deemer just shook her feathered head. *They cannae find them without the beasties!* But she had to go, so she spread her wings and headed out, looking for her pals.

~

Gee was peering to the south through the scope. Nothing. No vessels, no lights, just the deep blue sea glistening in the early morning light. He heard noises downstairs. Oh no, the family would be here, asking questions he could not answer. He let his shoulders drop. His feet felt like lead as he descended the stairs.

Pop was coming in the door, his arm close to his body and carried by the sling. He smiled at his friend, but there wasn't any mirth in it.

"Hey, Gee. Anything to report? I know the rest of the family has started to search. I thought I'd come here and hang with you."

"I'm afraid there's no news. The radio has been pretty silent until jist recently. The maritime authorities hav' resumed their search. But no sightings of the tramp cruiser." There was such sadness in his voice. It had been a long night, and he had no good news for his friend. If Socorro's light had gone out, the island would be devastatingly dark for so many.

"Well, let's go look from the tower. We can see for miles up there." Pop said, adjusting his arm sling.

The two men ascended the stairs. When they reached the observation tower, Pop handed Gee a thermos. "I brought tea. We'll have to scrape up breakfast later. I think Mary is working on it now."

CHAPTER 29

The Sea Turtle and the Rescue

Socorro and Rory sprawled out near each other on the sand. They gasped painfully as they caught their breath. *Now what?* The other lads slowly pulled themselves up and started scrounging around the boat, looking for food and water. But the desperate lads were becoming really greedy, fast! A fight broke out among them. The lads were cursing, and fists were flying!

Socorro and Rory watched the scene as if they were watching a movie. It was unbelievable, really. Socorro let out one of his shrill whistles by placing his fingers in his mouth and blowing with all his might! The lads stopped.

"Oi! Stop the nonsense. We all need what's in that boat, but we must be fair!" Rory called.

"Oh, yeah, and who do yous think you are to stop us?" Tad spat out. He took the stance of a professional boxer, legs apart and fists in the air in a fighting position. Socorro scowled. He didn't like Tad. He was bossy and mean. The minute they hit the beach; he'd been the one complaining loudest!

He shouldn't be surprised. It was obvious the lads were used to fighting for what they got off the streets. But he knew that fighting now would be detrimental to all of them.

"Well, you may think it's just the two of us against all of you, but it seems you've already forgotten about my friends, the wildlife! Socorro whistled again and a small flock of falcons appeared overhead. They swooped close to the angry lads, their sharp claws open and ready to fight! They came just short of grasping Tad's hair! They dove and screeched as the lads dispersed and ran!

"Stop! Call 'em off!" Tad screamed, as he swung at the birds.

They held their hands over their faces, trying to shield them from the predators. Socorro felt bad for them. He'd had his share of encounters with angry birds and knew just how it felt! But being outnumbered, this seemed the only way to get the lads to listen. "I'll call them off, but if you get violent again, I'll call them back!" he said through gritted teeth.

"Call 'em off! We'll cooperate!" Tad said.

Socorro waved his arms and signaled to the birds to stop. They made their final swoop, then rose to the heights of the crags. Socorro then waved a thank you to his loyal friends.

When they first came to the island, he had met his share of poachers and predators who were after the wildlife. But all the kids: Socorro, Kristal, Hamish and Ailsa, made it their mission to save the sea creatures and the exotic birds that were on the endangered list. And the animals hadn't forgotten their kindness!

Word traveled fast amongst the beasties, and even now, a couple of years later, they were still loyal. He had done a good thing when he helped God's creatures.

Tad brushed the sand from his clothes. He was at the end of his rag, seething with hate! *Those two will pay for this!* he vowed. But unless he wanted those wicked falcons attacking again, he must let them think they were in charge. "So, wha' ideas do yous have? You're naw gettin' all the food and water!"

"You're right, we donnae wan' it all. But we need to divide it evenly if we're goin' to survive. Spread the tarp and le's see wha' we've got." Rory instructed.

The lads reluctantly did as they were instructed. A wee mound of snacks, canned food and water dropped onto the tarp. But Socorro and Rory suspected that the lads had hidden some of it back. Socorro narrowed his eyes. "Listen, we play fair. If we find out you haven't, well, let's just say some of the beasties will return! Only this time they will do more than just send ya a warning!"

The lads looked at one another, their eyes large and fearful. A dozen more items dropped onto the tarp. Then they looked away, sheepishly.

"Great. I suggest we work together. If we spend all our time fightin', we'll use up energy that we need to survive! I say we make decisions as a team. Agreed?" Socorro asked them. They all nodded in agreement, albeit reluctantly.

The food and water were divided evenly amongst the seven lads. *If they consume it all at once, then it's each guy's choice.* Socorro understood that God gives us each a choice; it's up to us to choose wisely.

He pulled his phone from his back pocket. He shook it and pounded on the screen. It was supposed to be waterproof, but being exposed to sea water all those hours, it was toast! *Well, communication must be by beastie then!*

"Anyone have a compass or any idea where we might be? There are so many islands in the Scottish sea. We could be on any one of them." Socorro stated.

The lads just shook their heads; they'd been hostages on the *Sea Witch* and none of them owned a thing but the worn clothes on their backs! Not even a burner phone. Socorro shook his head. *Not good*.

He had no idea if they were still on *Mystic Island* or *Timbuktu!*

"If Hamish were here, he'd know. He grew up on the island and he knows every inch!" Socorro said to Rory. "Guess it's time to pray and ask God for guidance." Socorro didn't know if he should include the rowdy crew. But he invited them anyway.

"You think God cares one wee bit aboot all these orphans and misfits? I donnae. Pray if ya want, but it seems a waste of time to me." Tad shouted at him. But a couple of the others came over and said they wanted to pray. "Cannae hurt to try, might 'elp," said Boyd as he shrugged.

Socorro raised his voice so all of them could hear. But he didn't close his eyes. *He didn't trust these blokes.* "Dear Heavenly Father, thank You for taking us through the storm to dry land. We're dreadfully lost, but You know that, because You know everything. We really need to get home. Please guide us in the right direction! Keep us safe, and thanks for always being with us! In Your name we pray, Jesus, Amen."

Several of them called out "Amen."

Maybe just maybe the prayers for protection last night really meant something to some of them, Socorro thought.

"Look!" Jori shouted. "A sea turtle! He's beached over there."

The lads hustled over to where the huge turtle was stuck in the mud. It was alive, but just barely.

"Hey, can we eat turtles?" Boyd asked.

The turtle looked up at them, its eyes wide! "Donnae... eat... me!" He said, drawing out each word slowly.

The shocked lads gasped!

"No! I think it's a messenger. If I'm right, we'll be eatin' Mary's cooking soon!" Socorro said.

The turtle blinked its mammoth eyes and smiled. In a slow deep voice it said, "Aye, ... I'm... here... to... help... yous. I'll tell the whales... where yous are located. Wha' amazin' creatures... are the whales...! They communicate by sonar. They'll get word back to your family... fast! Wha' you've done for the sea beasties... has traveled far and wide!" He stopped and nodded his big head, then rested for a minute. "But... one... thing, I seem to be stuck here in the sand... Can you lads give me a boost... into the sea?"

The boys nodded. The turtle was huge, but with effort they should be able to carry it. Two got on one side and two on the other and hoisted the heavy beast enough to carry it into the sea. They shouted their encouragement as the turtle waved goodbye!

~

Meanwhile, hidden behind a stand of trees, a pack of hungry wolves watched them and licked their chops as they circled into a tight hunting stance. Their eyes narrowed and they lowered their heads as they concentrated on the prey. Those lads must be stopped! One of them in particular, Rory! He was dangerous and focused. They howled and scratched, their paws striking the ground as they flashed forward. But just as they were about to pounce, a tall dark figure stepped in front of them. She towered over the furry beasts, fire in her eyes. She lifted her sword and roared!

The wolves yelped and jumped back, cowering in front of the glowing form, Vesperinikin! They turned their tails and ran, the powerful spirit of good and all things holy, blazing after them. These demons could not stand before the angel of the One True and Holy King. And since the demons couldn't stop him, Rory was empowered by the Holy Spirit to speak the words that only God knew would help Tad the most.

~

Tad ran further up the shore and plopped down in the sand. He shook his head and hugged his body. *A talkin' turtle! I must have taken in too much sea water!*

Rory, although new at all this, saw this as an opportunity to talk to Tad. He sat down next to the lad as the others were exploring the island.

"I bet you're confused, and I get it. I was jist like you only a couple of weeks ago! God's spirit is strong here, and supernatural stuff happens. I know because of wha' happened to me! I was healed of all the pain I had endured in my life! Ya see, I'm an orphan, too, and like you, I was workin' on the *Sea Witch*. But one night, we veered off track and got close enough to shore that I saw a lighthouse! I grabbed a life ring and jumped into the sea!"

He glanced at Tad and he actually seemed to be listening. "I know it was crazy, but being desperate, I had no choice! And it turned out to be the best decision, believe me! Socorro is tellin' the truth, he lives in an enormous castle. They found me and took me in." —he swallowed, then continued— "The castle is brilliant! I even have me own room. But tha's nae even the best part. They have church in their parlor! I was forced to go, at first. Then God came and landed right here." Rory pointed to his chest. "I cannae tell ya wha' it means. Ya need to find ou' for yourself. It's no accident God saved us from the sea. Let Him save ya from your pain."

Tad looked away. He swiped a few angry tears from his eyes. The things Rory was talking about hit home. He, too, was filled with pain and anger. And yet, he couldn't deny the way they were saved from drowning in the sea. And, not just that, but the message from the sea turtle had to be from God!

He felt a stirring in his spirit. God was speaking to his heart. He looked up at Rory and cautiously nodded. Then he felt it happen. The heavy curtain that had covered him and kept him from seeing the light suddenly lifted. He felt the spirit come into his heart and he began to sob. Rory reached over and hugged him in a brotherly embrace until all his emotion was spent.

"Wow!" was all he could say. "I donnae wha' jist happened!"

"Well, I haven't learned enough of the Bible verses yet, but I know wha' God did for me! I believe the fact that you said 'yes' to his healin' means you believe He can change your life and tha's all that matters right noo. We'll be able to learn more, later. Wha' I do know is He will change us if we stop our old way of thinking and ask Him to make us new."

Tad nodded.

"The beastie went for help!" Rory said encouragingly. Then he stood up and signaled for Tad to follow him. It was time to catch up with the others.

~

In the shadows, Vesperinikin smiled. The creatures of the sea and the birds in the air all cried out in praise. The heavens rejoiced, as they always do when a lost soul is found!

There will always be wolves among us, *even on islands where they are not supposed to be*. But just as creatures of darkness exist, so do the creatures of light. Angels stand among the believers, helping them fight the battles. We are never alone. And we can be reassured that in the end we will win, because light always disperses the dark! We must believe with all our hearts and never, ever give up!

CHAPTER 30

The Beasties Save the Day

The snowy owl was on a mission. News of the lad's predicament spread quickly, and she was the one designated to tell the lighthouse keeper where the lads were! She flew rapidly over the sea, her three young owlets on her back. If it wasn't for Socorro and Ailsa, she would not even be here, with these, her second batch of owlets. She changed her course and tipped her wings to soar by the window where the two grandfathers were standing. The light caught her snowy feathers and gleamed through the glass, drawing their attention. She floated there long enough to make sure she was seen. Then she flew up to the top of the lighthouse and into the tower where she nested.

"Whoa! Did ya see that?" Pop asked. "A snowy owl and three owlets!"

Just then they heard the pounding of footsteps on the stairs. It seemed that the entire population of the island was rushing up. In reality, it was Kris, followed by the rest of the castle inhabitants. They had searched since daylight, but not finding any sign of the boys, they decided to come to the lighthouse. They crowded into the tiny room.

"Any sightings" Kris asked.

"Not of the lads, but a snowy owl was just here by the window. It was odd, it was like she wanted us to notice her." Pop said.

"She must have a message!" Ailsa was already on her way to the upper part of the tower. When she arrived, she scanned the rafters for the mother owl. She didn't see her! But as Ailsa watched, the owl landed on one of the highest rafters. After the owlets were snug in the nest, she flew down and landed near Ailsa's feet. Ailsa sat down, her legs crisscrossed as she leaned forward, so she could hear what the owl had to say.

"I have gud news! The lads are safe! They're on the island! Way over on the farthest side. But they need help to get home! The beasties sent me to tell yous. My owlets are too wee, and I cannae take you to them, but the whales are ready to show yous the way. Look into the sea, near the reef. You'll need a boat, but they'll guide you."

Ailsa jumped up, startling the poor bird. She drew back, flapping her wings.

"Oh, sorry, I didnae mean to scare ya. I'm jist so excited! How can we ever thank ya enough? Ta, is all I can say. Ta!" Ailsa disappeared down the stairs to the next level where the family waited.

"The lads are found! According to the owl, the whales will lead us to them!" Ailsa shouted breathlessly! "But we need a boat!"

The family hugged one another as they rejoiced! *Could it be true?* They were all talking at once, but they finally collected themselves enough to proceed. Gee used his cell phone to contact the maritime coast guard. He told them they had a strong lead and would fill them in later.

I must convince them to follow the whales, but how? Ailsa wondered.

Then the family gathered at the reef as they waited for the police boat. It took what seemed like an eternity, but finally a motor was heard as the boat sped into the bay. Hurriedly, they all boarded the vessel. As soon as they were all aboard, Ailsa hurried over to the coast guard officer who was giving out the orders.

"Excuse me, sir, but I know where the lost boys are!" The officer gazed at the girl, a quizzical expression on his face. "Aye," she said hurriedly, "they were spotted by some pals of mine. See the whales lined up ahead?"

The captain gazed into his telescope, and he saw several whales waving their tales just ahead of them in the bay. *Rather unusual to see them in these waters*, he thought. His interest piqued, he turned to the lass.

She continued. "I know this is going to sound weird, but the whales will guide us to the exact location where the lost lads were seen. Look, they are slowly pushing ahead. They want us to follow!"

For some unknown reason and against better judgment, the captain gave the crew the orders to follow the whales. If nothing else, they could reassess the situation when they got into deeper waters. But to his amazement, the majestic creatures led the vessel through the bay and into the mystic waters of the Scottish sea! *Hopefully the lass knows what she's talking about!* He had no time or patience to waste on wild whale chases!

CHAPTER 31

HOME AT LAST

The lads were perplexed. The place seemed to be deserted. *An unknown island somewhere*? If so, they hoped the creatures would be able to help them. They wandered around a bit, enjoying the rays of sun on their backs. But the clouds were forming overhead. If they were drenched again, the cold may be their undoing.

"While we wait, I think we should make a shelter from the tarps. Look at the clouds! We need to stay as dry as we can. I know I'm not wanting to get soaked again!" Socorro said.

The lads ran to the lifeboat. "Let's get in the boat and cover ourselves with the tarps like we did yesterday," Boyd suggested. They got under the protective tarp just in time. As it always does in Scotland, the rain poured down. The thunder crashed around them. But the tarp kept the dampness out. It was dark and claustrophobic, and the poor blokes grew uncomfortable in the tight quarters.

"Let me tell you about something that happened to me on *Mystic Mountain*." Socorro said, hoping to pass a bit of time. "I was there with my sister Kristal, and my parents on a camping trip. But we were hopelessly lost on that mountain, because an earthquake had split our family up. We were lost for days and days and at one point, I slipped on this muddy slope and fell! I was headed right off a cliff! But just as I reached the edge, I grabbed hold of a branch. I tied myself on to it and hung on tight! The river below me was so far away, it looked like a snake. Another earthquake or aftershock shook the tree I was tied to, and it fell! Crashed to the ground!" Everyone listened carefully, fully engaged in the story. Socorro continued.

"Somehow, I was thrown over the trunk and I straddled it, safe on the ground! When that quake knocked over that tree, I was sure I would fall to my death!! But I believe I was saved by that earthquake. I wasn't a believer at the time, but after that, I knew that God had a purpose for me. And more than that, He cared enough about me, that He saved me from death. I turned my heart to Him, then. I know that it seems hopeless right now, but the same God that saved me from the fall from the cliff and who saved us from the storm last night is here with us now. Honestly, he even saved me from a dragon!"

The lads were hanging on every word. They needed the hope that God was with them. They needed to be found!

"Wait, wha' did ya say aboot a dragon?" Rory asked.

Socorro told them about his capture, the battle and the rest of the story of the things that happened on *Mystic Mountain*. He knew he was setting himself up for ridicule. But he'd decided a while back that being honest was more important than being liked by his pals.

The lads were so intrigued with the story they lost track of time. The thunder drowned out the sound of the rapidly approaching speed boat. They were startled when the tarp was pulled away from them and they were surrounded by a group of people! There were several men in uniform, Hamish, Ailsa, and the rest of Socorro's family!! They were quickly escorted to the police boat and brought on board. They wrapped them in special thermal blankets and gave them cups of hot tea to drink on the way back to the castle. On the way, Socorro asked them, "Did you find the captain and the rest of the crew of the *Sea Witch?*"

"Not yet. If they are out there, the helicopters will find them. But we will be interested in your stories. I understand you were taken aboard against your will?" the police captain asked.

"We were!" Jori cried out.

"By the stormy sea, he knabbed us," Thomas said, raising his fist and nodding. Then all the lads were talking at once, excited and ready to tell of the injustices that were forced on them.

"Wait!" the police captain shouted. "Once you've rested, we'll get written statements from each of you."

"Let's get you lads home, fed, and in warm clothes, first.

"Rory, I have wonderful news for ya! Your pup, Brandi, made it home. She is safe and sound with Foster and the other pups that haven't been given away yet. A fox helped her after she got lost from you." Ailsa said.

"Yes!" he said as he pumped his fist in a victory signal.

"I'm thankful she's alright. I've thought of little else once we were safe on land. I cannae believe we were captured by modern day pirates! If it weren't for the quick thinkin' of Socorro, I bet we wouldnae be here noo. But we'll tell ya all aboot it soon."

~

At the castle, the weary lads filed into the parlor. Mary told them there was a hot meal waiting. She hugged Socorro and Rory, teary-eyed, while Brandi and Foster gave them a good licking!

Socorro and Rory got the gang warm jumpers and a change of clothes for each of them to wear before the meal. Getting dressed next to the roaring fire was a luxury they hadn't had in ages.

The exhausted lads began to yawn as fatigue and hunger set in. Socorro used the walkie-talkie to request that their food be brought upstairs as he showed the boys to their rooms. They led them to the next floor up, where the rooms were standing ready. The rooms were for the hired hands, when they were there. Nothing fancy, but they were all private, clean, and better than the lads had ever seen!

The weary boys thanked their hosts and disappeared into their rooms. Trays filled with hot mashed tatties and fried fish, were brought up by Mary and Ailsa. Steaming cups of tea and honey and a big bowl of peach cobbler finished the meal.

Ailsa stopped by Socorro's room on her way back to the kitchen. "I'm so thankful you're home!" She blew him a kiss and quickly tip-toed out the door.

CHAPTER 32

FALL FESTIVITIES

It was noisy at breakfast the next morning. The recently rescued lads were excited and overwhelmed at the hospitality they'd received and the majesty of the castle. Socorro promised to give them a tour soon, and Hamish promised to show them the lighthouse, and how it worked. Ailsa whined that she and Kristal better be treated special since they were so outnumbered, being the only girls.

"Wha'? You're already treated like royalty, I'd say! And as it should be," Hamish said as he winked at Kristal. She blushed and ducked her head.

The lads were much more pleasant after the breakfast and the good night's sleep than they were when Socorro first met them. But surviving a storm changes a person. And being treated like royalty themselves didn't hurt!

Gee joined the family for breakfast, so Ailsa and Socorro didn't have to bring his food to the lighthouse. But as soon as they had finished, the maritime police showed up to take their statements.

The lads painstakingly wrote out their complaints. It was then the police informed them that they found the pirates and had them in custody. Socorro was glad they'd made it through the storm, even if they were criminals. There was still a chance for them to change.

Rory hurried upstairs to find Brandi. He wanted to take her for a wee walk around the premises.

Socorro helped Ailsa feed the sheep. They chatted non-stop, Socorro updating her on his adventure.

The festival was tonight! There were still lots of things to do to get ready.

Kristal went upstairs to the room that she and Ailsa now shared. When she opened the door, she was met by Ailsa's kitten, Dacey, who was having a *disco party*! As the giant ball spun, the sun rays gleamed from each tiny square, causing the light to dance across the floor of the room. The cat did her best to catch each spot. She jumped from one to another, mesmerized by the reflections. Kristal laughed at her antics! She decided, then, to forget about hanging the heavy drapes back up, and enjoy the light from the window. She arranged the rest of the room to her liking, then took photos to turn in to her professor at Uni. She hoped she would get a good mark for her design.

Kristal found her parents in the yard, putting out the final decorations. The castle garden had to be ready since the musicians would be performing in the garden.

Hamish, Rory and the other lads were busy decorating the flatbed trailer, getting it ready for the parade. It was piled high with hay and pumpkins. Orange and white lights hung from the sides and there was a small pen set up in the middle. Curious, Kristal inquired about who would be in the pen.

Hamish scooped her up and said in a deep voice, "It's for you, my dear!" He swung her onto the flatbed where the other lads pretended to push her into the pen! Kristal squealed and they all fell onto the hay, laughing!

"So, who will *really* be in the pen?" Kristal asked again as she climbed out.

"I'm thinking it's for the rest of the wee pups that still need a home." Tad said.

"Well we'd better get back to work! It's only an hour until we ride in the parade!" Rory warned.

Socorro and Ailsa ran over to help.

"The lads will sit on the hay bales and toss candy to the wee tots. But we need a scarecrow! Who shall we pick?" As one voice they yelled out "Socorro!"

Who better than he to shoo away scary birds!

Kristal convinced him to go to her room so she could apply the needed makeup for a proper scarecrow.

As the evening approached, Pop backed the tractor up to the flatbed and hitched it up. The float riders climbed aboard. When everyone was in place, he chugged away. The riders rocked through the potholes and laughed as they fought to stay aboard!

Kristal smiled. She thought Socorro made a great Scarecrow, and Ailsa made a cute crow, fluttering around him. Five yapping pups rode in the center pen. The rest of the lads tossed sugary treats to the kids, those treats that didn't disappear in their own mouths, that is! Grammy led Foster, who was dressed as a pumpkin, down the village street as they too, participated in the parade. Kristal passed out balloons to the village children.

That evening, after the parade, the music festival began in earnest. The entire village attended! It was cold outside, but the warmth of family and friends, mixed with random fire pits scattered about, helped them deal with it. It was definitely the highlight of the season.

On the way home, Ailsa hopped out and threw all of the leftover veggies that had collected in the bin to the waiting beasties.

"Why, thank yous so much!" Lulabelle mooed out.

"NO, thank you!" Ailsa shouted. "I know you were a part of the beastie chain that helped us find the lads!"

"Aye, tis true," the wee calf Belgium cried.

The parade and festival had been a huge success. Many of the shop owners had decorated floats in the parade and the island guests had lined up along the road to see the beautiful entries. Even all the puppies found 'furever' homes.

CHAPTER 33

EASTER

In the Spring, it finally grew warm enough for one of the biggest events on the island. Easter sunrise service. Most of the villagers were in attendance that day. It was still dark as they gathered on the beach near the lighthouse. They waited quietly for the imminent sunrise.

A young minister from Edinburgh waited up to his waist in the cold sea waters. He was surrounded by puffins, dolphins, whales and almost every sea creature you can imagine. The wild ponies watched from the lofty rock crags. Sea birds circled the group as their cries echoed in the still darkened sky. The snowy owl and the peregrine falcons were perched nearby.

As the first rays of the sun peeked over the horizon, Ailsa entered the water, followed by her dad, Murdock. Then the other new believers waded in to wait their turns for the believers' baptism.

Mr. Mark beamed as the Liverpool lads entered the waters, followed by Rory, Hamish, and Gee.

Then a brief prayer of thanksgiving was offered before they were all baptized one by one. Those on the shore shouted and clapped. as he watched all the baptism.

They'd gone through some very tough times, all of them. But now, together, they were going through the mystic waters of baptism.

Adara and Mary grabbed hands and looked at one another. God had not only saved their families; He'd healed each of them in a miraculous way! They smiled at each other as they savored the amazing things God had accomplished on this island!

After the waters were stirred by all those following after Jesus' example of baptism, a great cloud of color filled the sky! Hundreds of wee hummingbirds danced into formation.

"Look, Kristal," Ailsa shouted.

"Yes, it's the hummingbirds from *Mystic Mountain!*"

"I see what ya mean! It is a bit of heaven that were seein'!"

But they weren't the only ones celebrating the baptism! Another creature from Mystic Mountain appeared. Adara gasped as she saw Vesperinikin, the enormous creature discovered on the mountain. She stepped forward, her long ebony hair blowing in the breeze. She began to sing in her beautiful voice, *Amazing Grace!* Soon they all joined in, the heavenly music touching one and all.

Socorro felt a nudge as the red foxes brushed under his hands. Kris was surrounded by the white bunnies they had come to know on the mountain, their coats shining iridescently in the sun.

Many "laughing" pikas (they sounded like babies when they laughed) and several fat beavers (who waved to everyone), filled the beach.

Then Kris' heart leapt at the sound of galloping hooves. Lakota, the majestic white horse they had met on the mountain flew in, her long white mane blowing in the wind. Sitting astride the magnificent animal, was Yazzie, the raccoon and behind him sat Sam, the angel. He had appeared to them in the body of a Native American and was adorned in his native costume, complete with feathers tied in his hair.

Tears ran down Kristal's face as she gazed at him, the man who had led them up and out of Mystic Mountain. It was a reunion of the best sort, from the mountain to the island. They were all there, all of them, the creatures wee and tall.

But it wasn't over yet! The sky lit up as the many pastel bats came into view. There were lots of oohs and awes with their arrival!

Sam, sitting perfectly still on the shiny alabaster horse, turned his gaze toward the highest point on the rocky ridge. They all followed his gaze.

There, shining brilliantly, was the One True King; The cougar the Frazier's met on the mountain. He stood there majestically; His jeweled crown glimmering in the sunlight! The One True and Holy King!

He was king of the mountain, and He was king of the island, but most importantly, He was king of their hearts. His radiant light shone brightly on *Mystic Island* and gleamed through the *Mystic Waters*. It pushed away the darkness, as only light can. And in the quietness of the moment, they all bowed their heads before Him, thankful for all He had done.

But sometimes, in the deep ink of night, the mysterious red eyes can still be seen lurking around the castle. And it's then that they realize that the battle is not over. They understand and so must we, to be forever diligent to trust the One True and Holy One who watches over us all! He will come again, and when He does, He will overcome all evil!! Then we, (all those who are His), will dwell in His house forevermore!

The End

Epilogue

After Hamish and Kristal finished their studies at the Uni, they returned to the island to work. Kristal was now a full-time interior designer. She worked with a firm in the city, who allowed her to work remotely. This allowed her to spend all the spare time she could, designing the rest of the unfinished rooms in the castle. She updated the decor in the common areas and made it all more comfortable for their many guests. She was also the wedding coordinator for those who chose the island to "tie the knot". She knew she had found her niche.

Hamish was now a meteorologist and astronomer. He worked with Gee, who was beginning to slow down some, due to his advanced age. He still lived and worked at the lighthouse, but he was glad to have Hamish there to take over on long stormy nights.

As a newly married couple, Hamish and Kristal lived in the attached cottage of the lighthouse. They would soon welcome their first child and there were plans for building on a few extra rooms to accommodate their growing family. And yes, Ailsa had been chosen to be a bride's maid in their wedding!

Rory had finished his preparatory studies and was now attending a Seminary in Edinburgh. He was becoming quite the orator and was known as a great soul winner in the city. He had met a young lass in his classes, and it was rumored that they might be needing Kristal's wedding planning services, when their studies were complete.

Socorro was studying veterinary medicine. He had several more years before he was ready for practice, since he was planning on combining that occupation with marine biology. Perhaps he chose that career opportunity because the love of his life, the beautiful curly-haired Ailsa, was already studying to be a marine biologist! They planned to return to the island to work and study in the newly rebuilt animal research center.

And most likely, wedding bells will ring in the near future, for this couple as well. Ailsa had accepted and wore Socorro's lovely engagement ring!

Castle Rossmore had evolved each year since the Frazier's had been there. It went from a vacant stone building to a place God had used as a resting place for travelers and for those who needed to draw close to Him. Now, it had become a full-time boarding house for orphaned children. Only one floor held holiday guests, and the rest of the thirty-five bedrooms were filled with lads who no longer had families or homes.

As time went by and many of the lads decided to stay there, an American teacher was brought in to oversee their schooling and training. Mr. Mark proved to be the perfect man for the job. He was compassionate, but also strong enough to handle the sometimes-unruly youth. He had trained many men to be roughnecks in his past career in Oklahoma, USA, so this lot was no match for him. But he was also well studied in the Bible and shared his faith with the blokes, daily. His influence was life changing for many of the lads. It wasn't long until they thought of him as family.

The light continued to shine brightly through the *Mystic Waters*, guiding the lost to find their way home. And in the stillness of the evening a song could still be heard as it rose on the breeze...

The earth shall soon dissolve like snow, the sun forbear to shine; But God, Who called me here below, shall be forever mine.

Amazing Grace - John Newton

ABOUT THE AUTHOR

I hope you've enjoyed the Mystic series. I pray that these books have touched your life in a positive way.

You can find more of my writing at tabathaswaybright.com.
If you are led to, please give me a review at Amazon and Good Reads.
Blessings!

www.ingramcontent.com/pod-product-compliance
Lightning Source LLC
LaVergne TN
LVHW090517110826
845146LV00003B/886

* 9 7 9 8 9 9 0 0 5 3 7 2 4 *